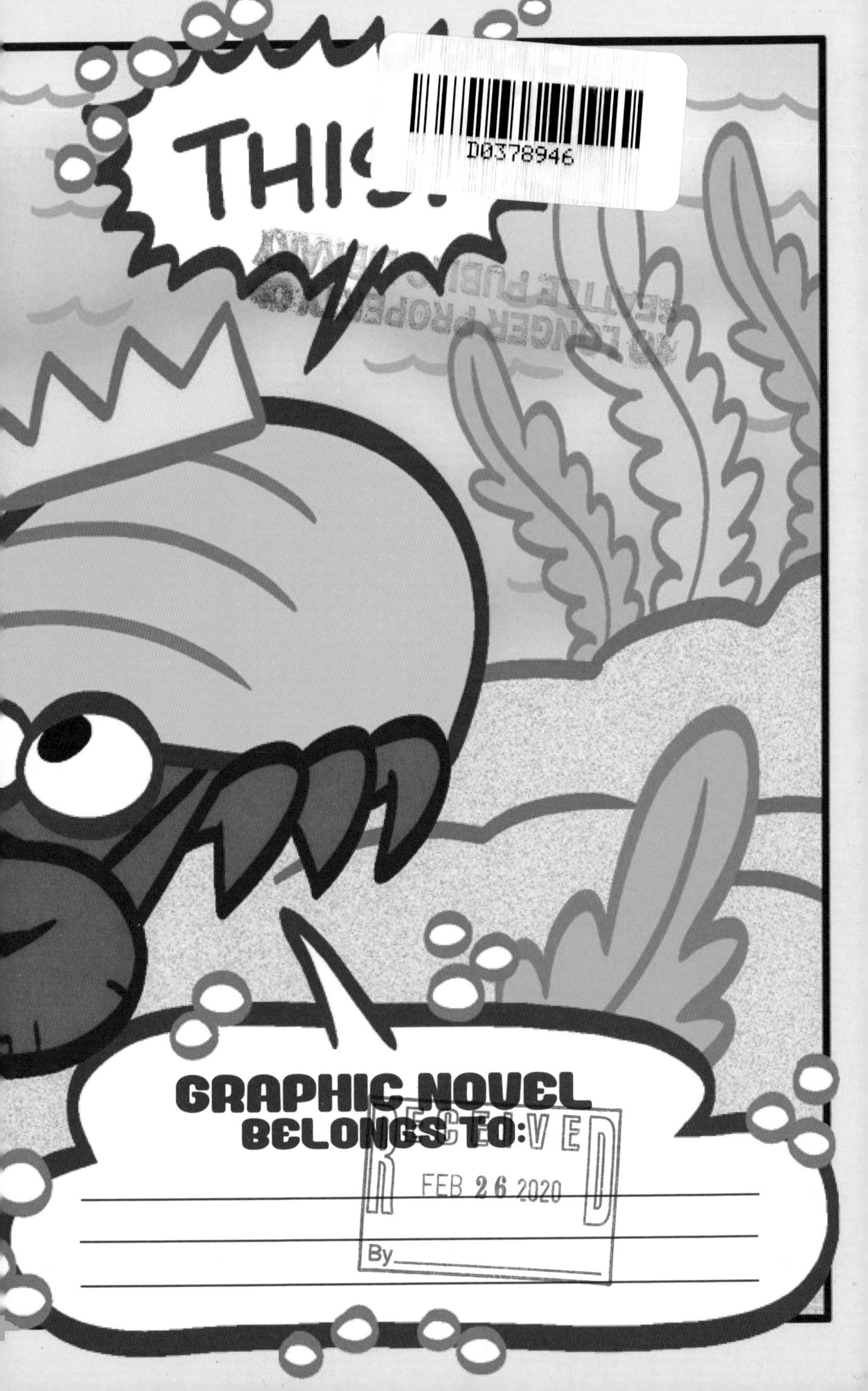
THIS
GRAPHIC NOVEL
BELONGS TO:

GILLBERT

BY ART BALTAZAR

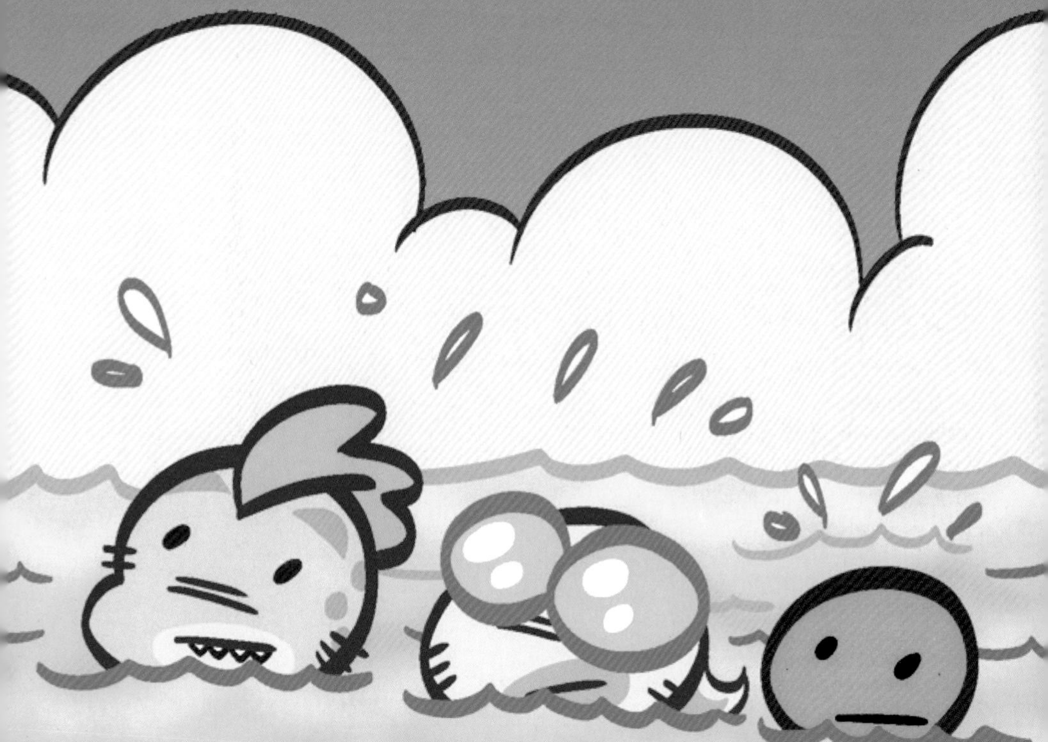

THE CURIOUS MYSTERIOUS

PAPERCUTZ
NEW YORK

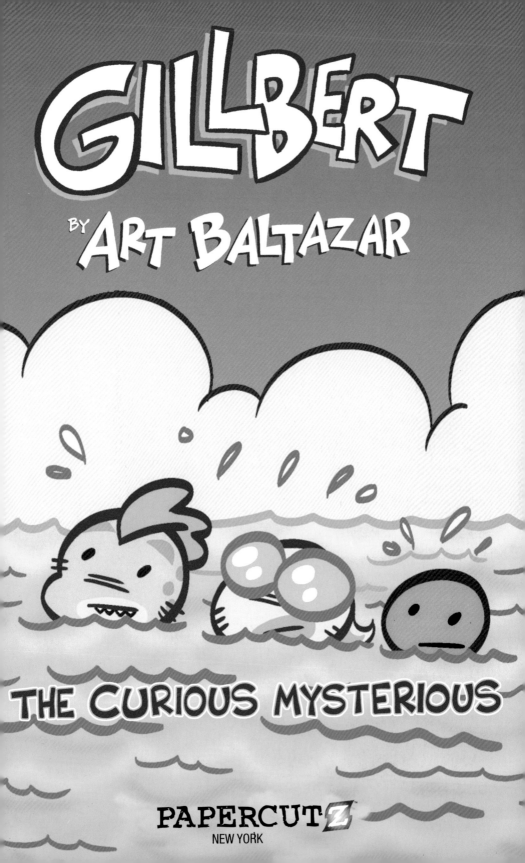

Here's what you missed in  #1 "The Little Merman"

Underwater, Gillbert, the young prince of Atlanticus, discovers a message in a bottle with his turtle best friend Sherbet. Only problem? Gillbert can't read. He needs his mom to translate it. While waiting for the translation, Gillbert and Sherbet see a mysterious mermaid lurking around and follow her. She leads them through the current of communication bubbles deep down to the submarine party of Wewillrocktopolis. There, she reveals her name is Anne Phibian and introduces them to her partying fishy friends. Meanwhile, deep in space, a fiery asteroid is on a collision course with Earth along with some flaming space invaders named Pyrockians. It lands on the ocean floor. The asteroid is actually an egg and King Nauticus and the Queen Niadora raise it like their own child. They name her Matilda. But this baby grows and grows and grows out of control. Back at the party, Anne teaches Gillbert to communicate telepathically and takes him to meet the mysterious space creature, Teeq, in her crashed space shipwreck. Teeq shows Gillbert her communication control center where she makes contact with intelligence from beyond our galaxy. She is attempting to make contact with her long lost sister. After a busy night, Gillbert falls asleep and wakes up back at the palace. Things heat up when fiery Pyrockian invaders invade the ocean, increasing the ocean temperature. King Nauticus struggles to hold off the invasion. Matilda returns to send to a warm volcano to call their own. Teeq shows up to the kingdom letting the King and Queen know that Matilda is actually her sister. The queen recognizes Teeq as her old friend and a celebration is in order. Gillbert never did see that his message in a bottle said he was destined for greatness.

GILLBERT

#2 "The Curious Mysterious"
By Art Baltazar
Production – Big Bird Zatryb
Managing Editor – Jeff Whitman
Jim Salicrup
Editor-in-Chief

Papercutz books may be purchased for business or promotional use. For information on bulk purchases please contact Macmillan Corporate and Premium Sales Department at (800) 221-795 x5442.

Hardcover ISBN: 978-1-5458-0348-6
Paperback ISBN: 978-1-5458-0349-3

Printed in Turkey
January 2020

Distributed by Macmillan
First Printing

SHERBERT   ANNE PHIBIAN   GILLBERT   KING NAUTICUS

AW, YEAH! PAPERCUTZ PRESENTS...

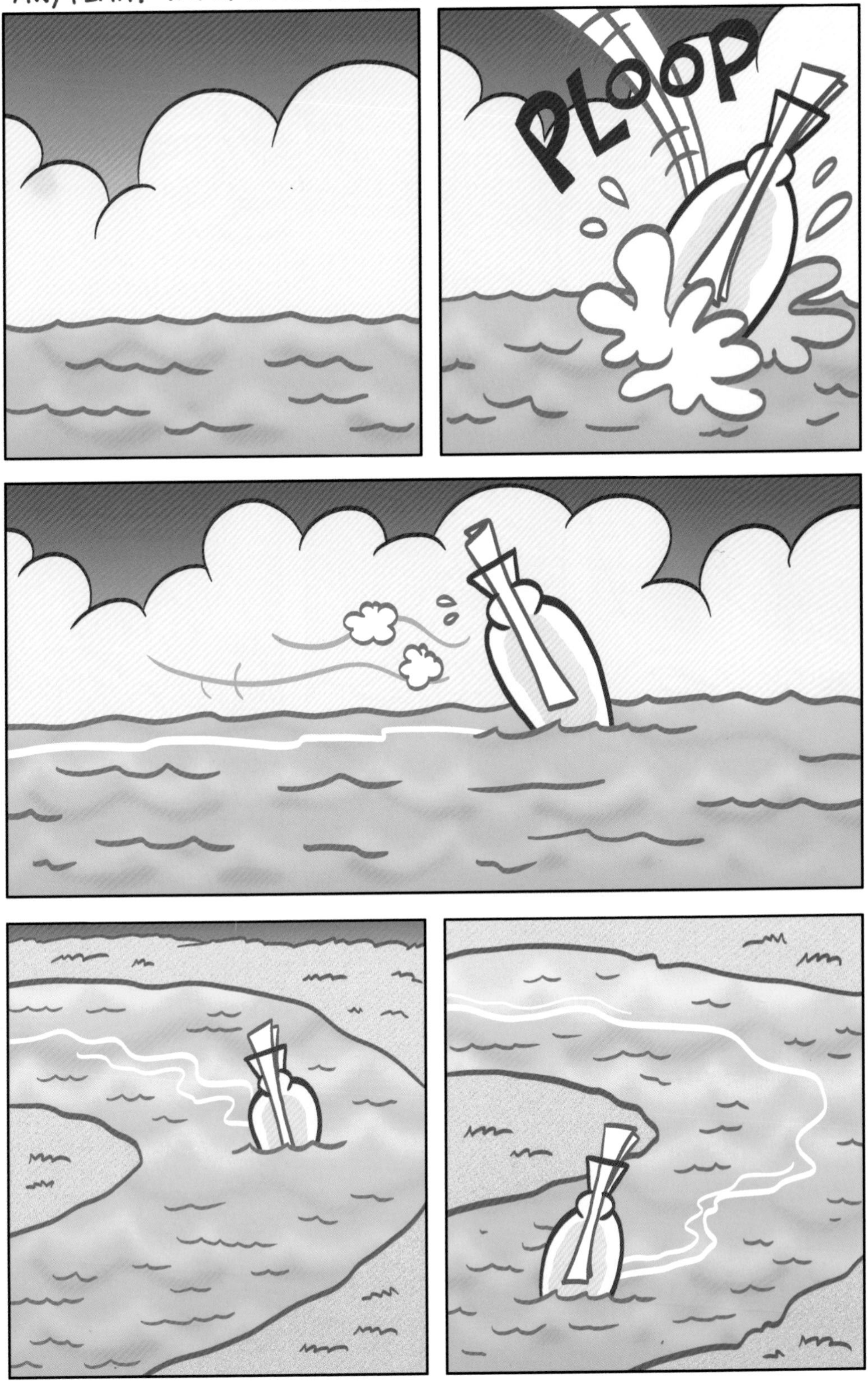
PLOOP

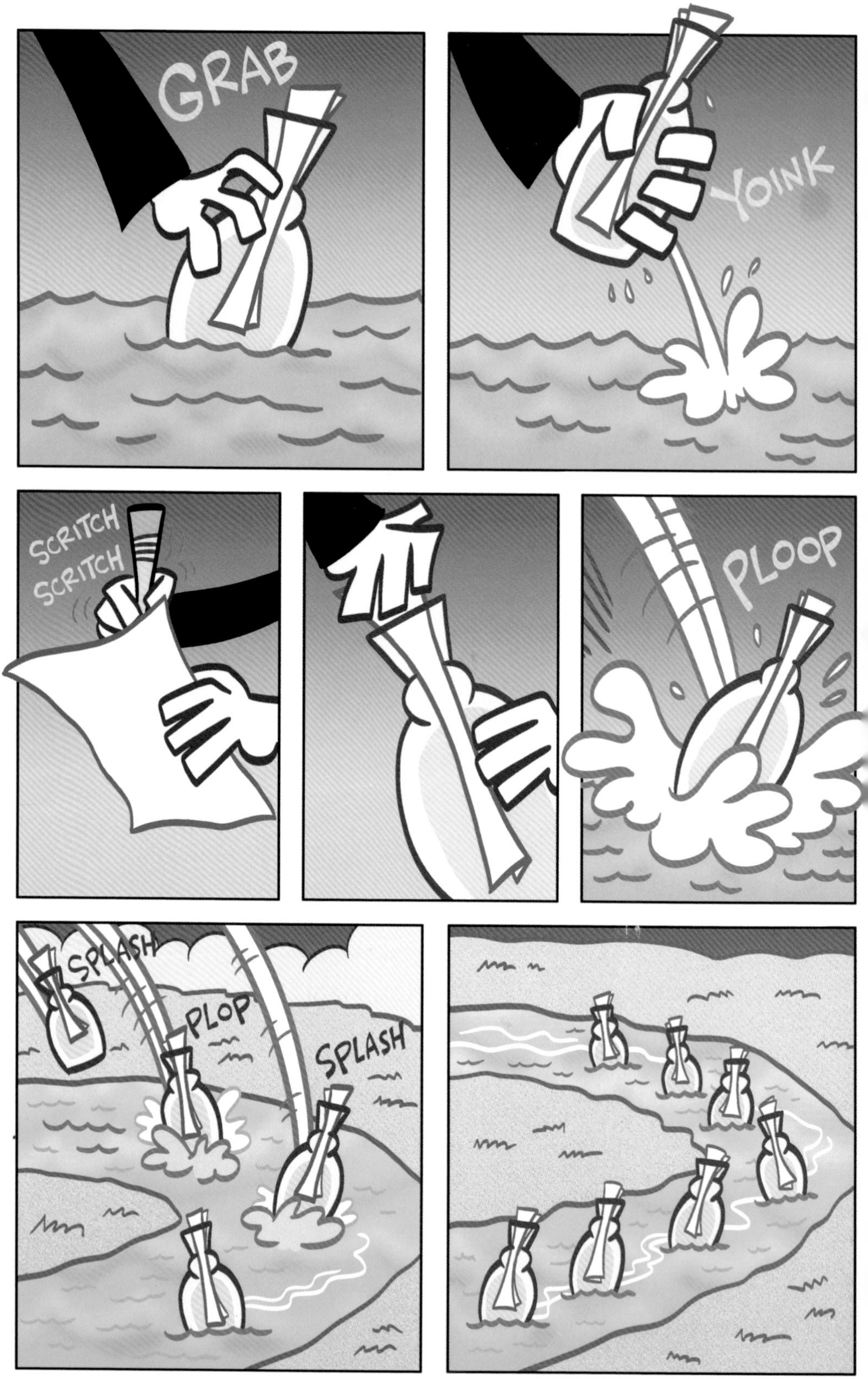
GRAB
YOINK
SCRITCH
SCRITCH
PLOOP
SPLASH
PLOP
SPLASH

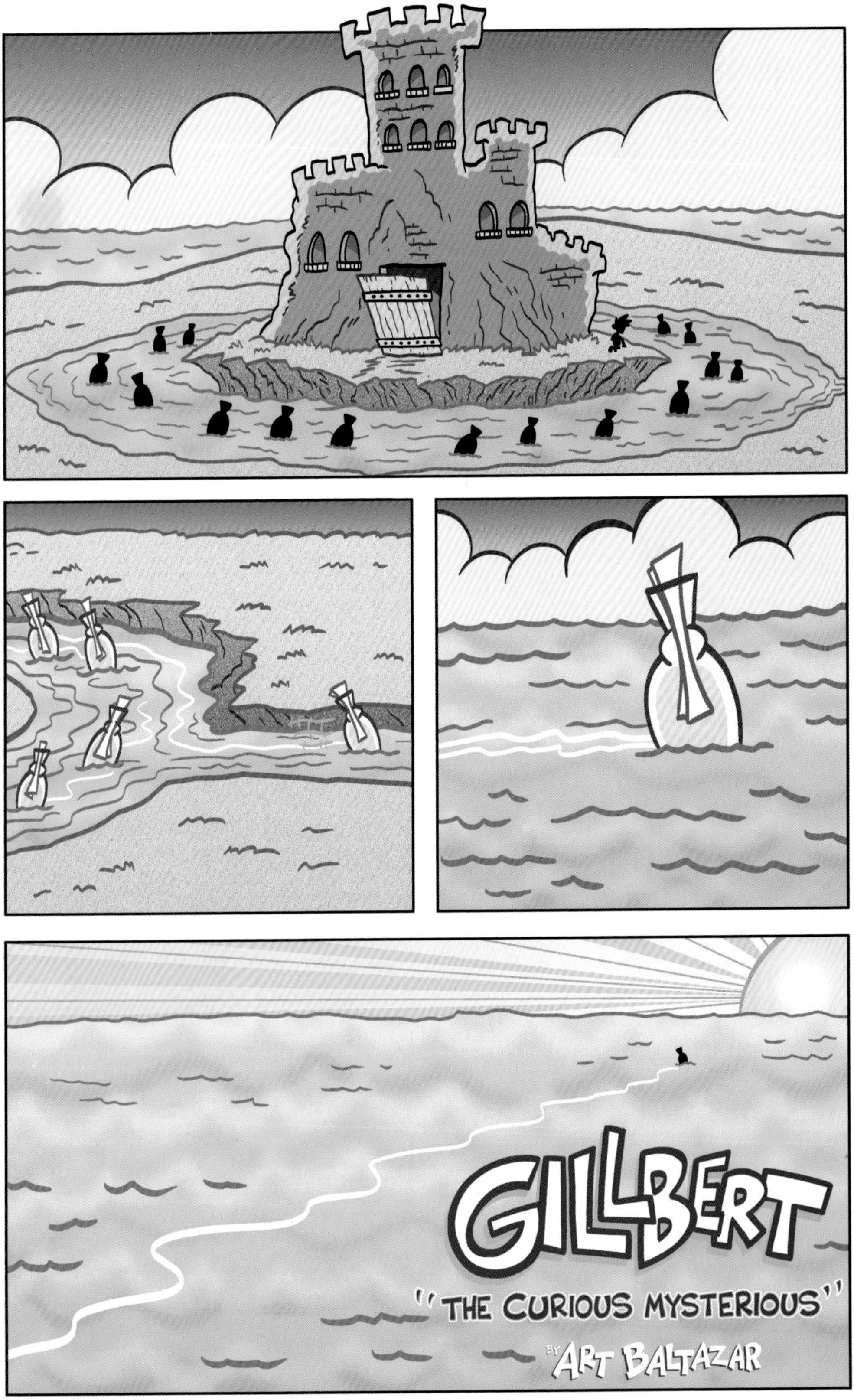
GILLBERT
"THE CURIOUS MYSTERIOUS"
BY ART BALTAZAR

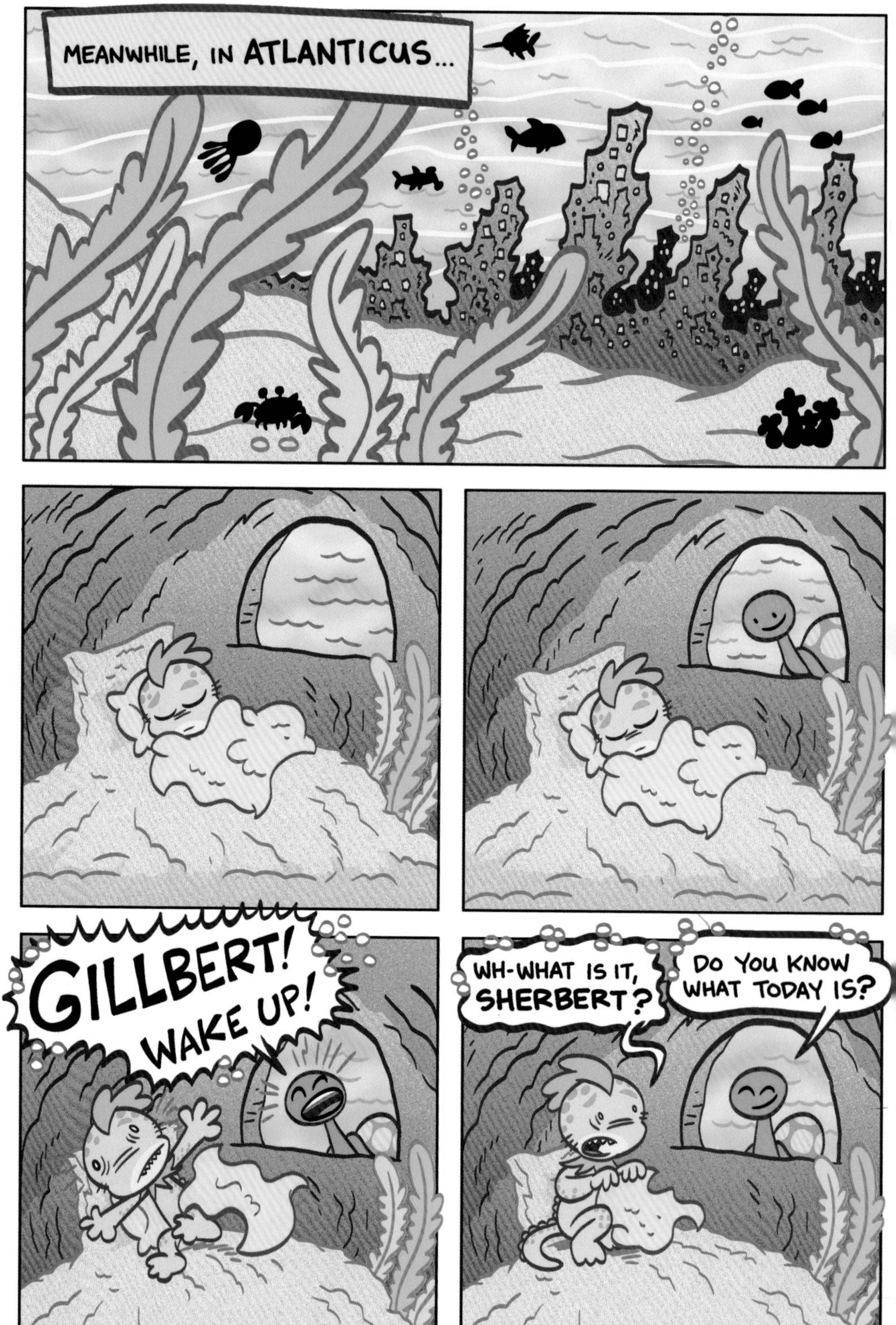
MEANWHILE, IN ATLANTICUS...
GILLBERT! WAKE UP!
WH-WHAT IS IT, SHERBERT?
DO YOU KNOW WHAT TODAY IS?

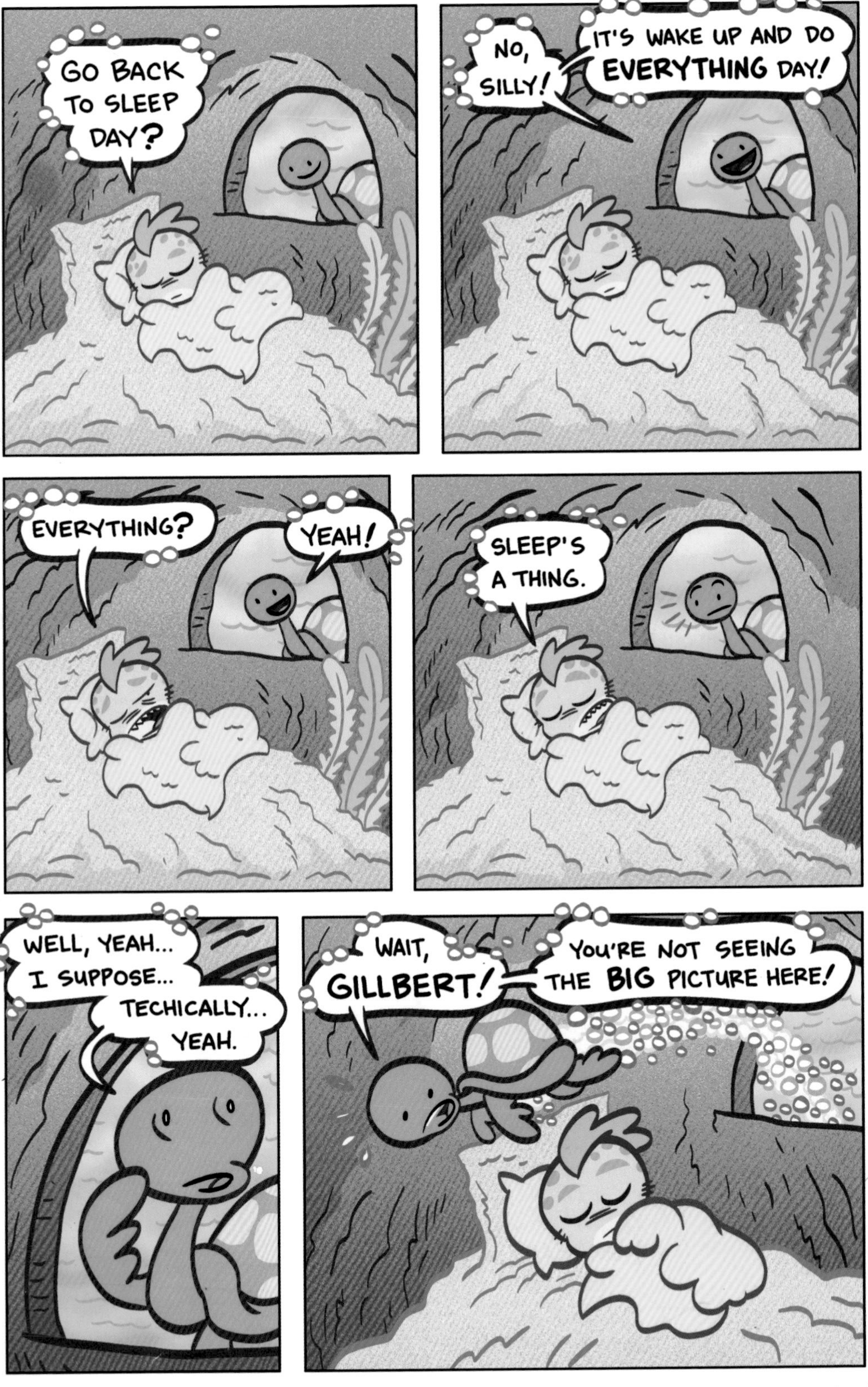
GO BACK TO SLEEP DAY?
NO, SILLY!
IT'S WAKE UP AND DO EVERYTHING DAY!
EVERYTHING?
YEAH!
SLEEP'S A THING.
WELL, YEAH... I SUPPOSE...
TECHICALLY... YEAH.
WAIT, GILLBERT!
YOU'RE NOT SEEING THE BIG PICTURE HERE!

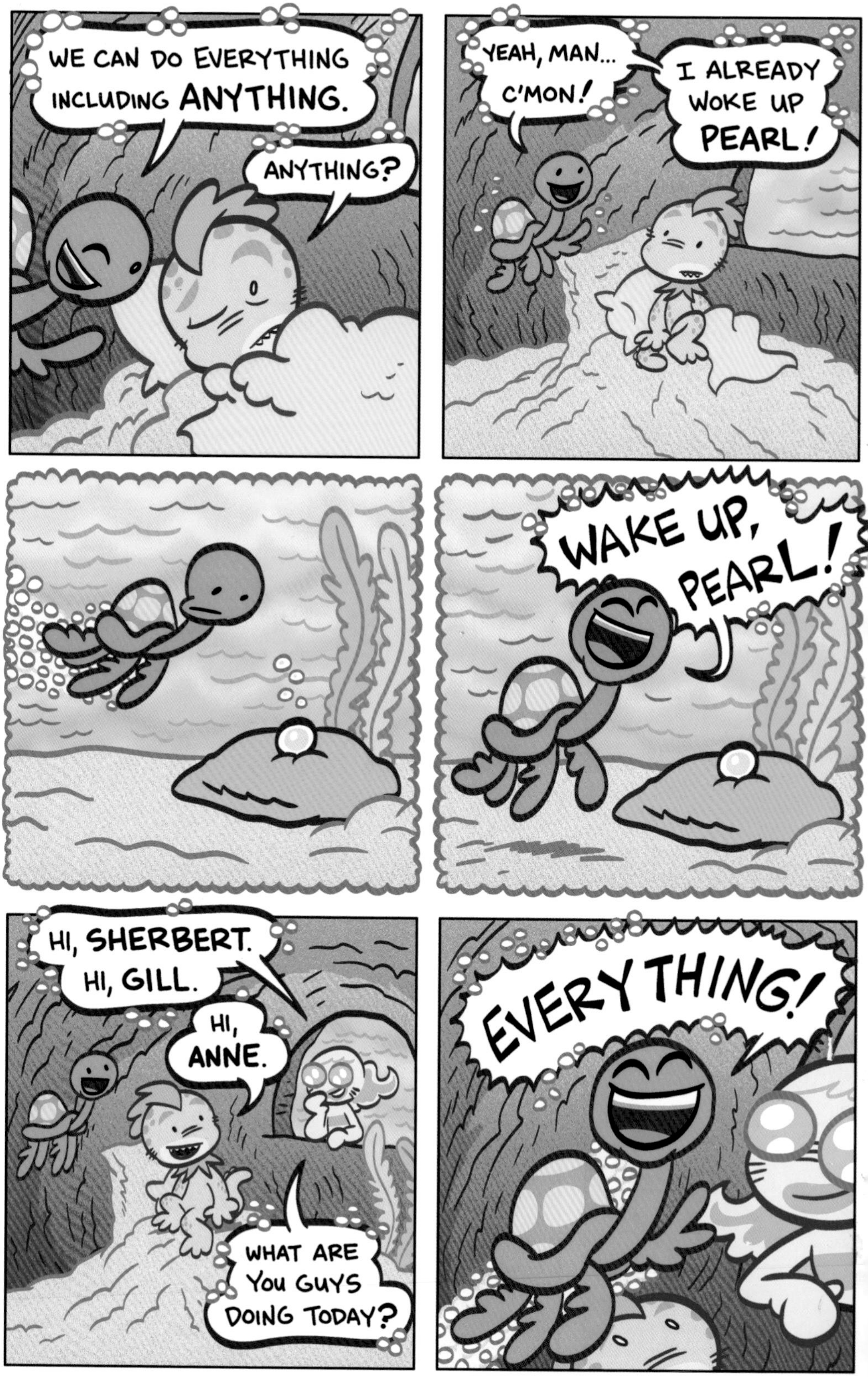
WE CAN DO EVERYTHING INCLUDING ANYTHING.
ANYTHING?
YEAH, MAN... C'MON!
I ALREADY WOKE UP PEARL!
WAKE UP, PEARL!
HI, SHERBERT. HI, GILL.
HI, ANNE.
WHAT ARE YOU GUYS DOING TODAY?
EVERYTHING!

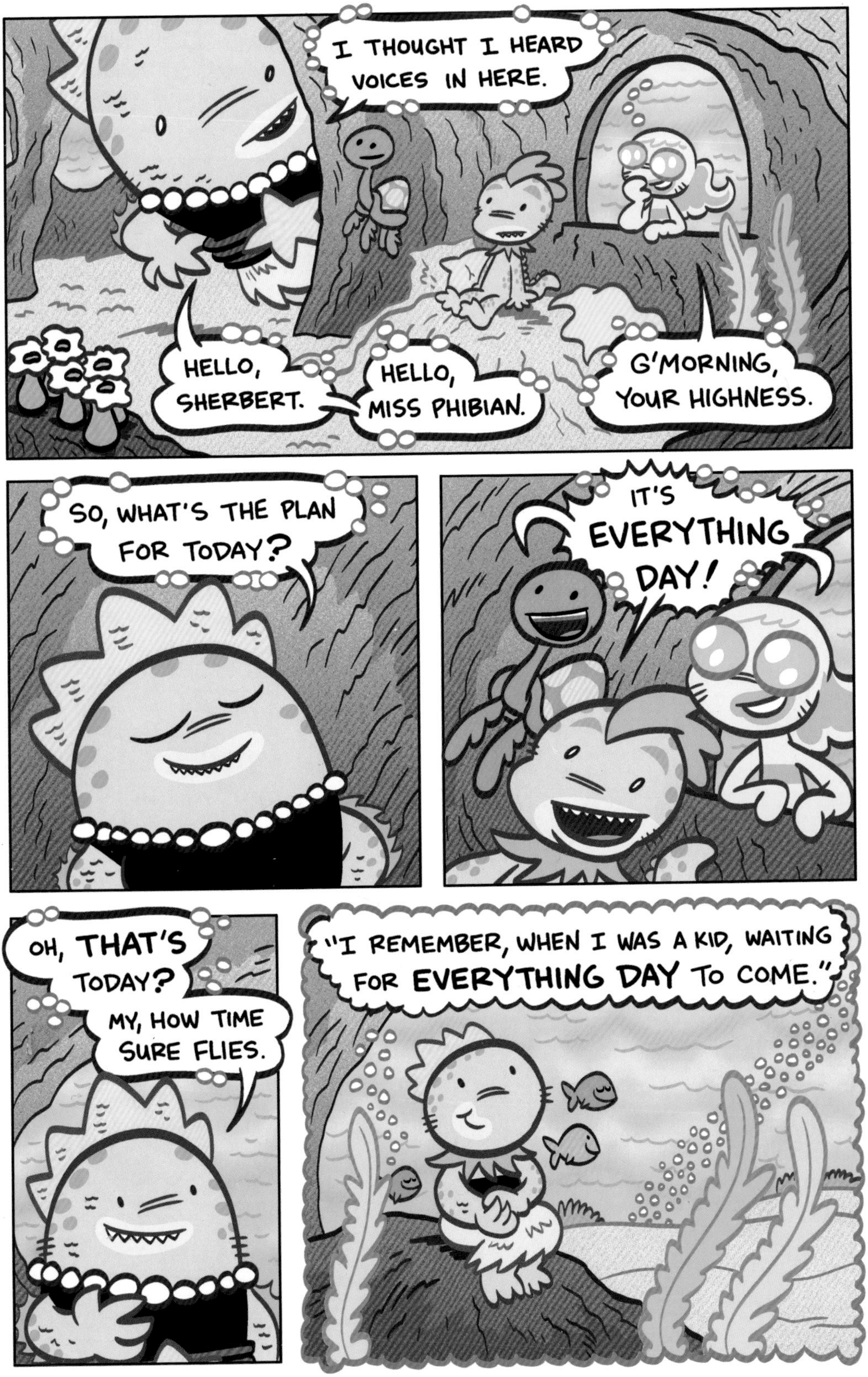
I THOUGHT I HEARD VOICES IN HERE.
HELLO, SHERBERT.
HELLO, MISS PHIBIAN.
G'MORNING, YOUR HIGHNESS.
SO, WHAT'S THE PLAN FOR TODAY?
IT'S EVERYTHING DAY!
OH, THAT'S TODAY?
MY, HOW TIME SURE FLIES.
"I REMEMBER, WHEN I WAS A KID, WAITING FOR EVERYTHING DAY TO COME."

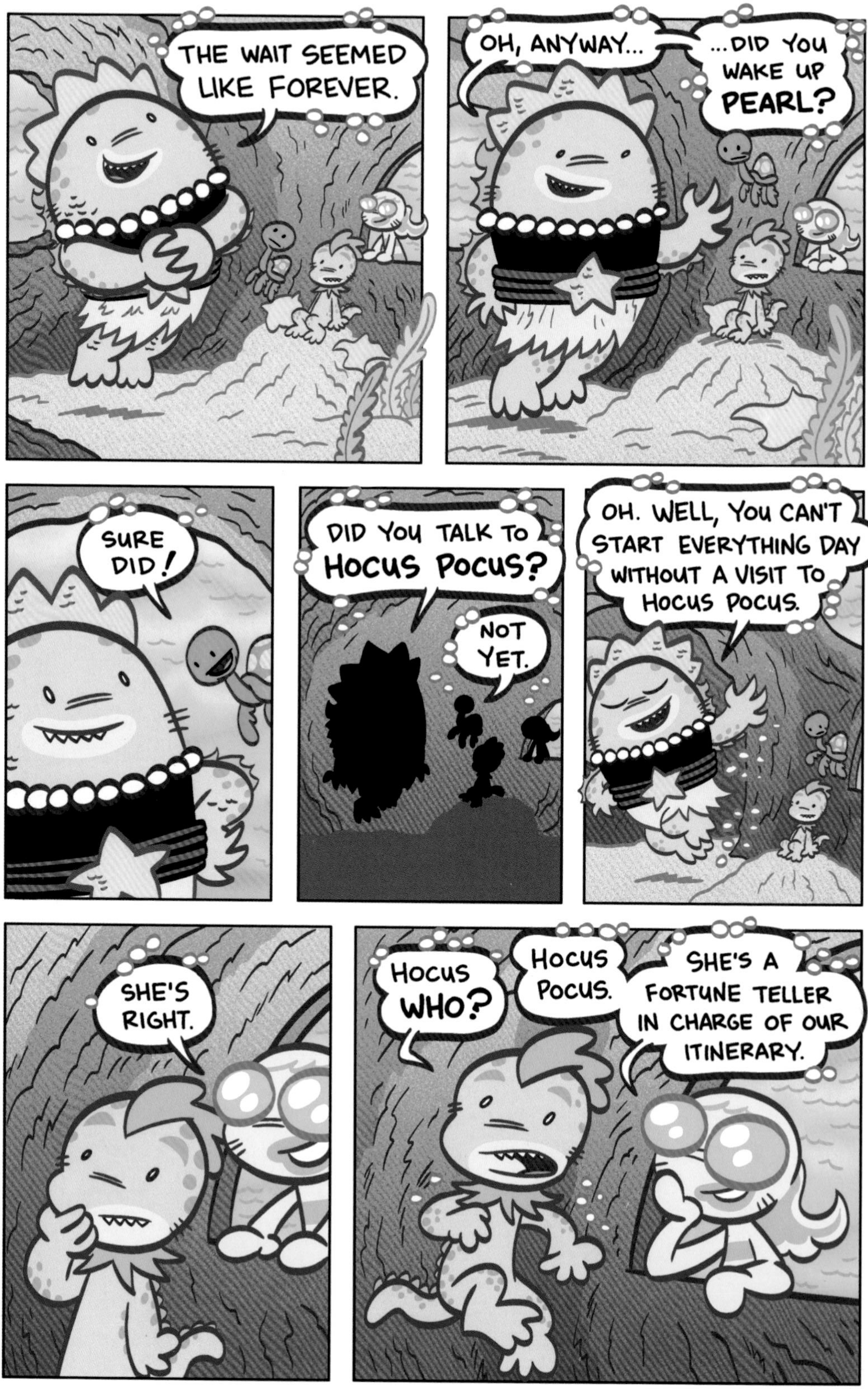
THE WAIT SEEMED LIKE FOREVER.
OH, ANYWAY...
...DID YOU WAKE UP PEARL?
SURE DID!
DID YOU TALK TO HOCUS POCUS?
NOT YET.
OH. WELL, YOU CAN'T START EVERYTHING DAY WITHOUT A VISIT TO HOCUS POCUS.
SHE'S RIGHT.
HOCUS WHO?
HOCUS POCUS.
SHE'S A FORTUNE TELLER IN CHARGE OF OUR ITINERARY.

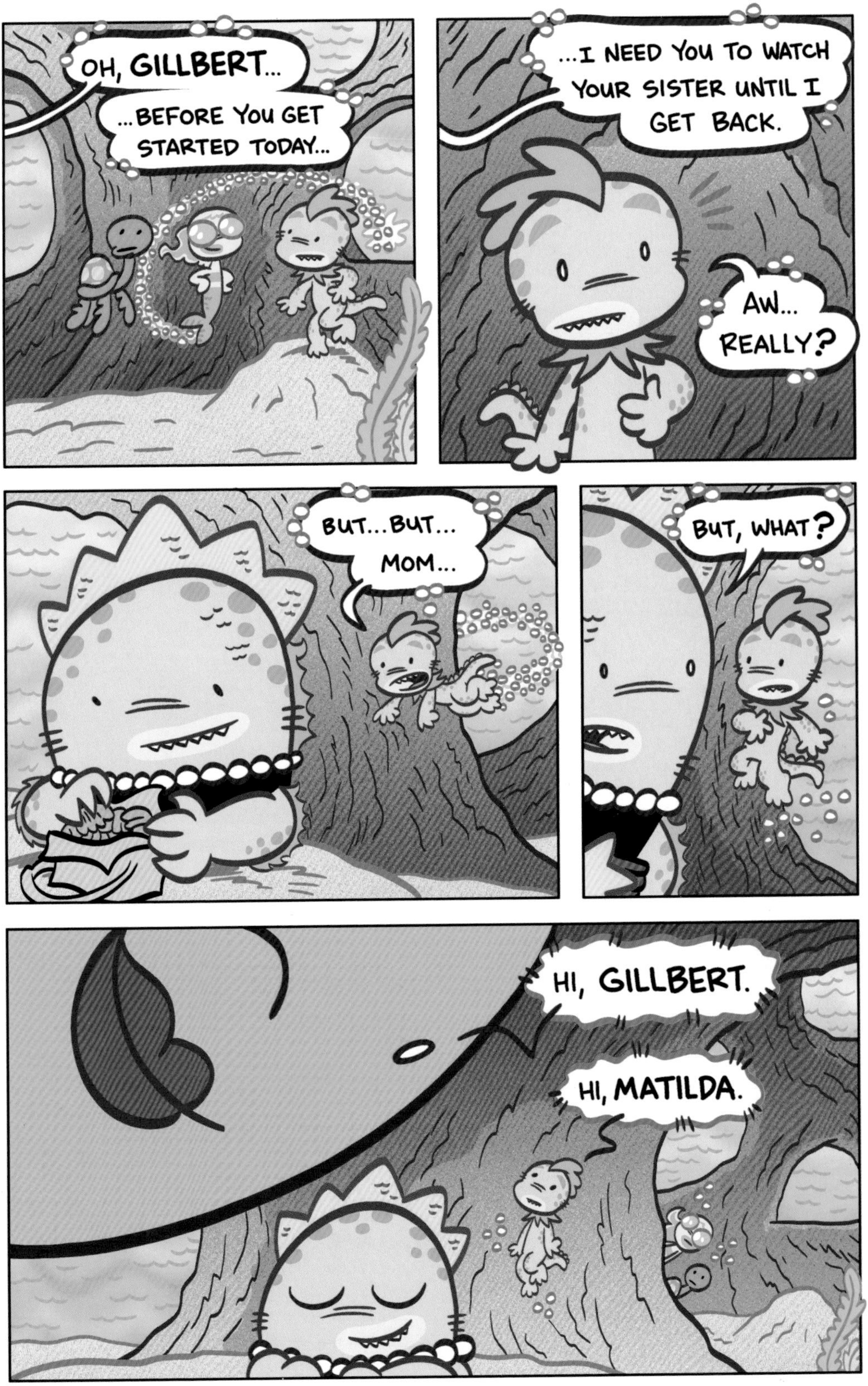
OH, GILLBERT...
...BEFORE YOU GET STARTED TODAY...
...I NEED YOU TO WATCH YOUR SISTER UNTIL I GET BACK.
AW... REALLY?
BUT...BUT... MOM...
BUT, WHAT?
HI, GILLBERT.
HI, MATILDA.

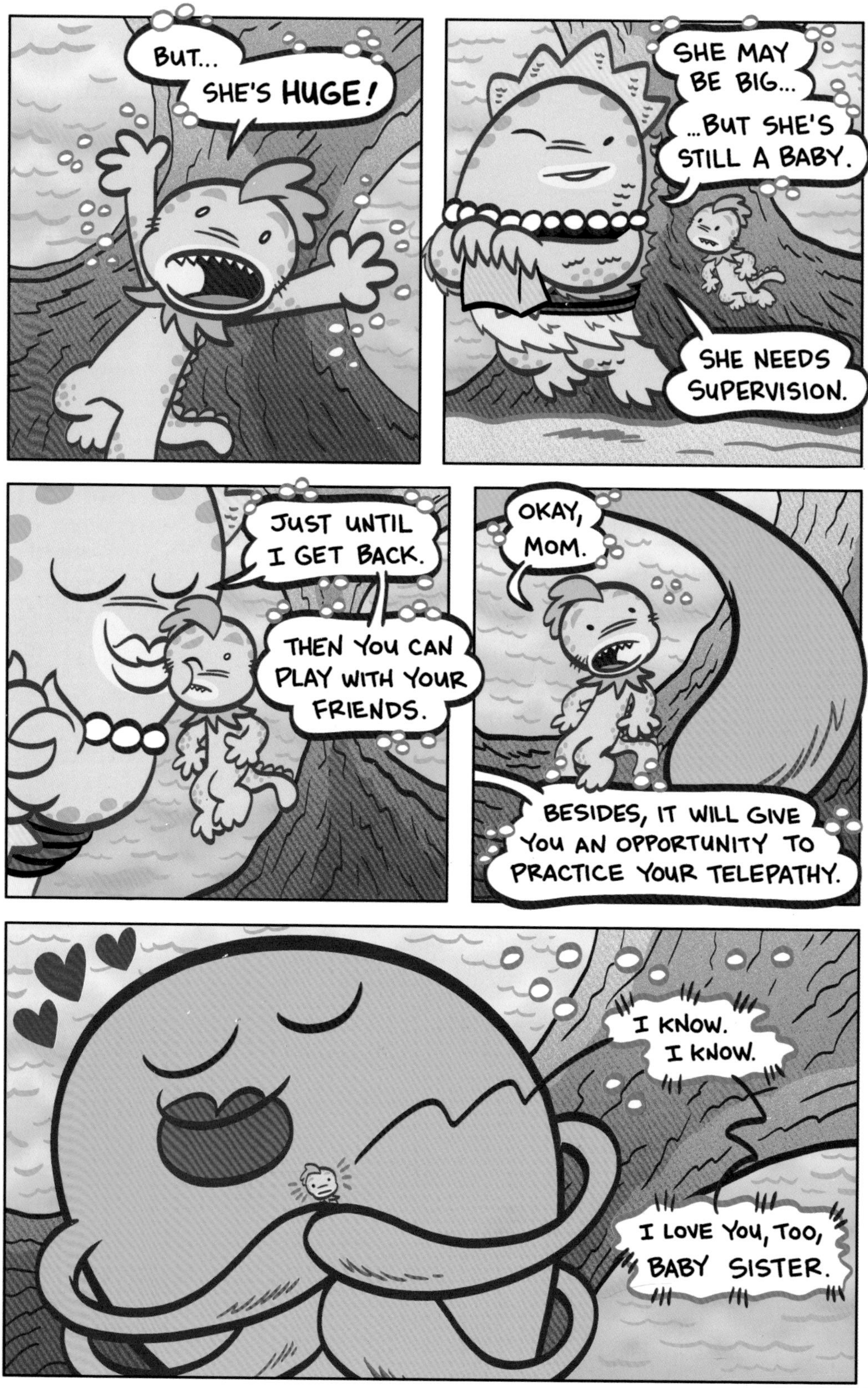
BUT...
SHE'S HUGE!
SHE MAY BE BIG...
...BUT SHE'S STILL A BABY.
SHE NEEDS SUPERVISION.
JUST UNTIL I GET BACK.
THEN YOU CAN PLAY WITH YOUR FRIENDS.
OKAY, MOM.
BESIDES, IT WILL GIVE YOU AN OPPORTUNITY TO PRACTICE YOUR TELEPATHY.
I KNOW. I KNOW.
I LOVE YOU, TOO, BABY SISTER.

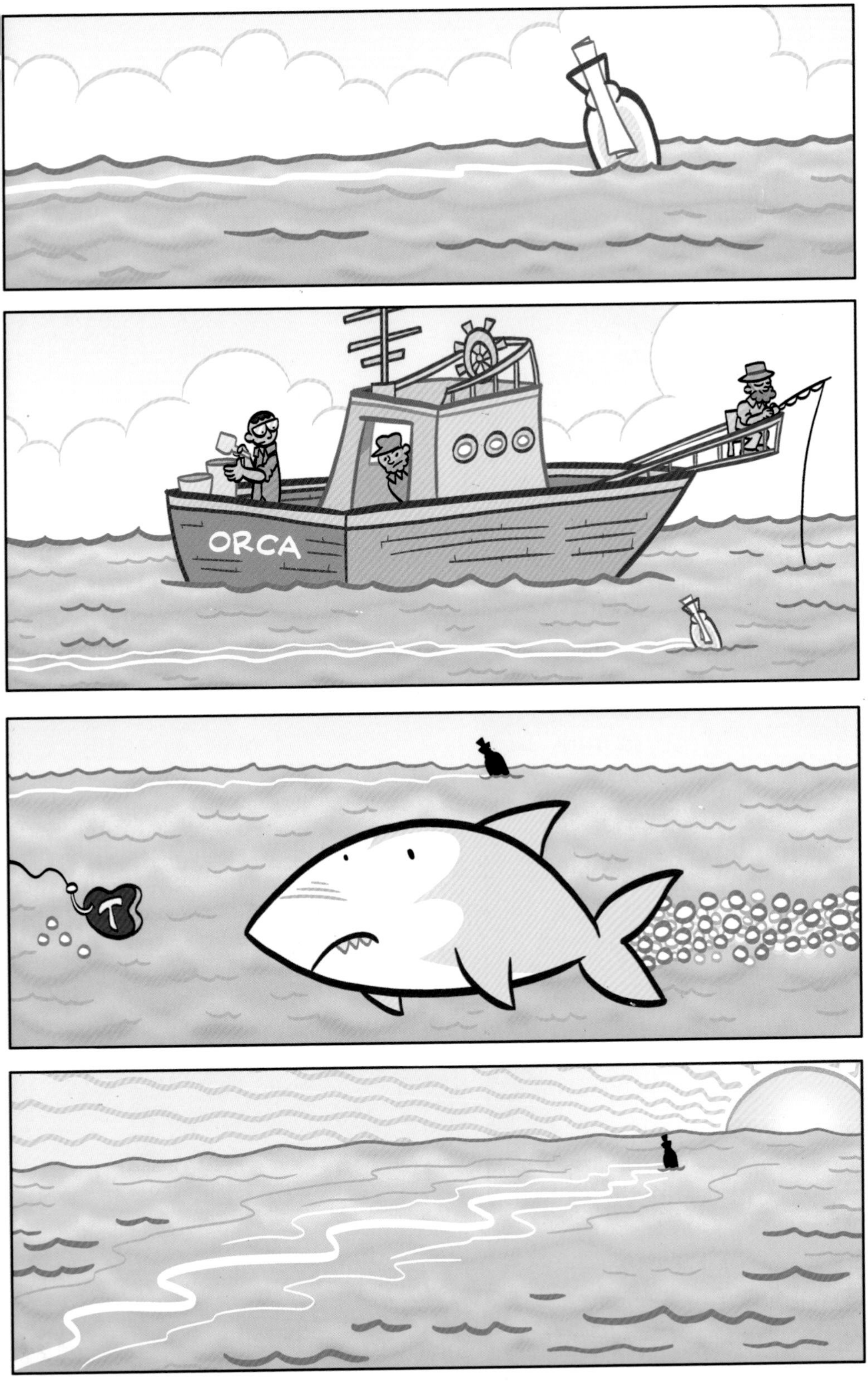
ORCA
T

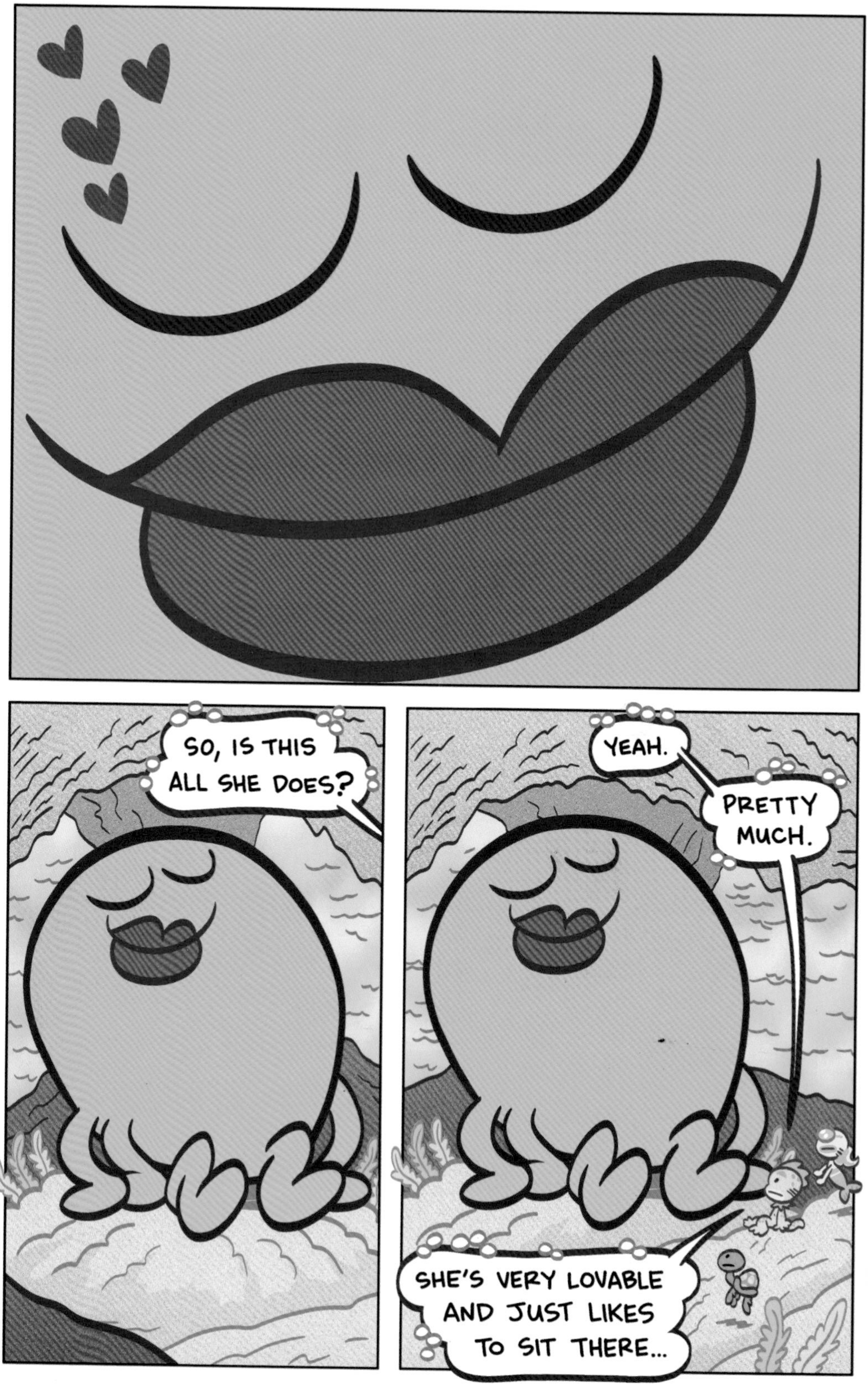
SO, IS THIS ALL SHE DOES?
YEAH.
PRETTY MUCH.
SHE'S VERY LOVABLE AND JUST LIKES TO SIT THERE...

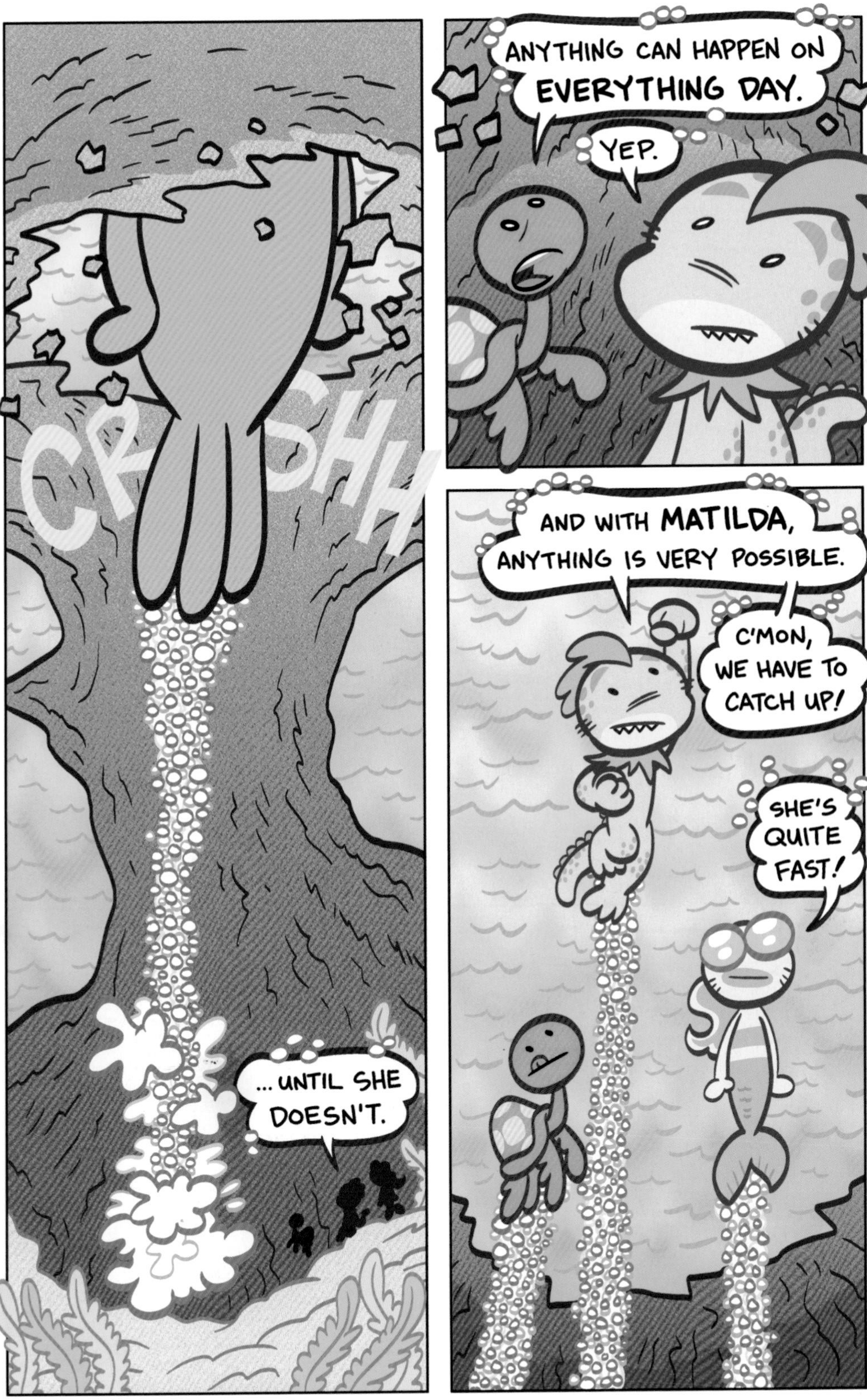
CRSHH
...UNTIL SHE DOESN'T.
ANYTHING CAN HAPPEN ON EVERYTHING DAY.
YEP.
AND WITH MATILDA, ANYTHING IS VERY POSSIBLE.
C'MON, WE HAVE TO CATCH UP!
SHE'S QUITE FAST!

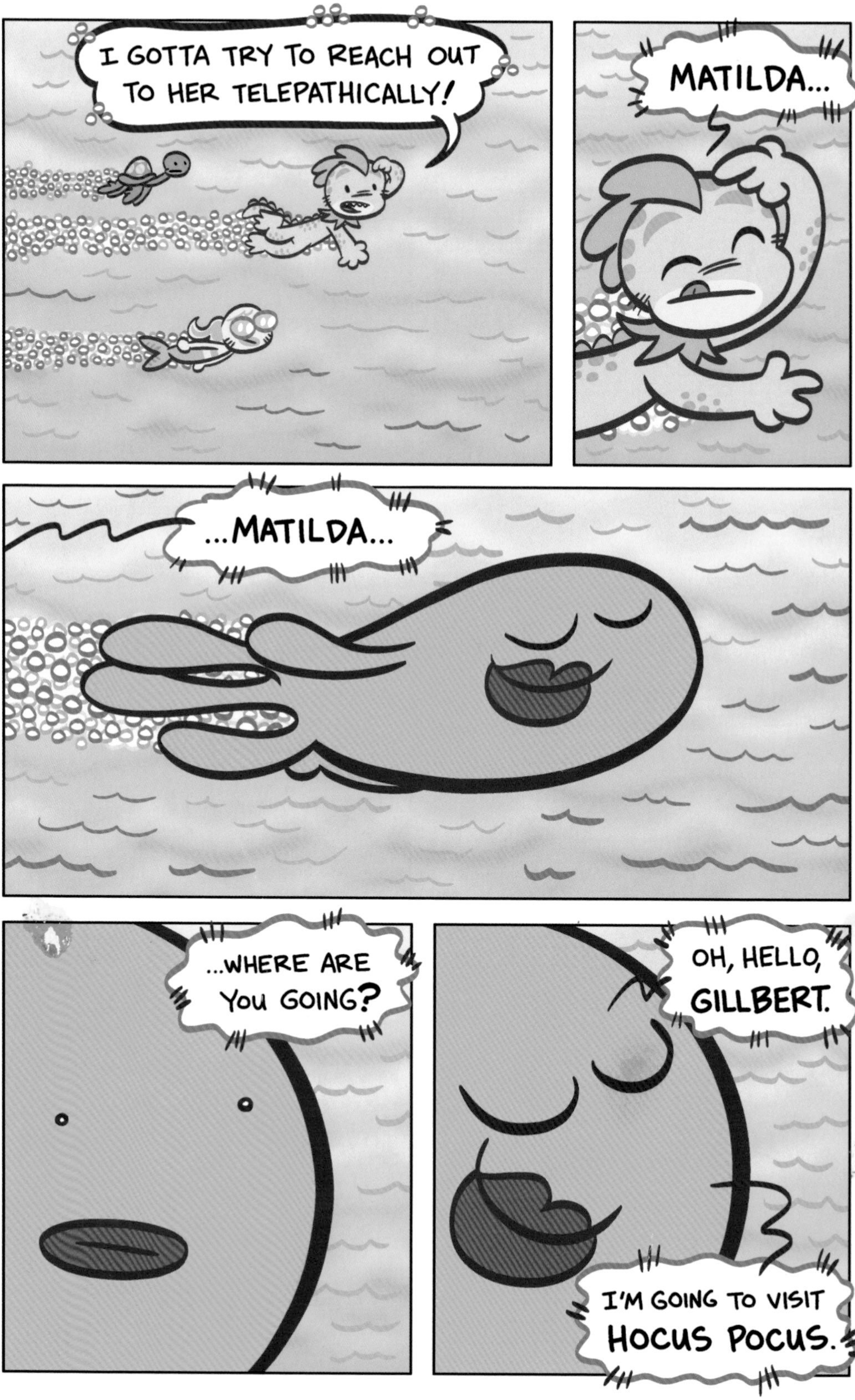
I GOTTA TRY TO REACH OUT TO HER TELEPATHICALLY!
MATILDA...
...MATILDA...
...WHERE ARE YOU GOING?
OH, HELLO, GILLBERT.
I'M GOING TO VISIT HOCUS POCUS.

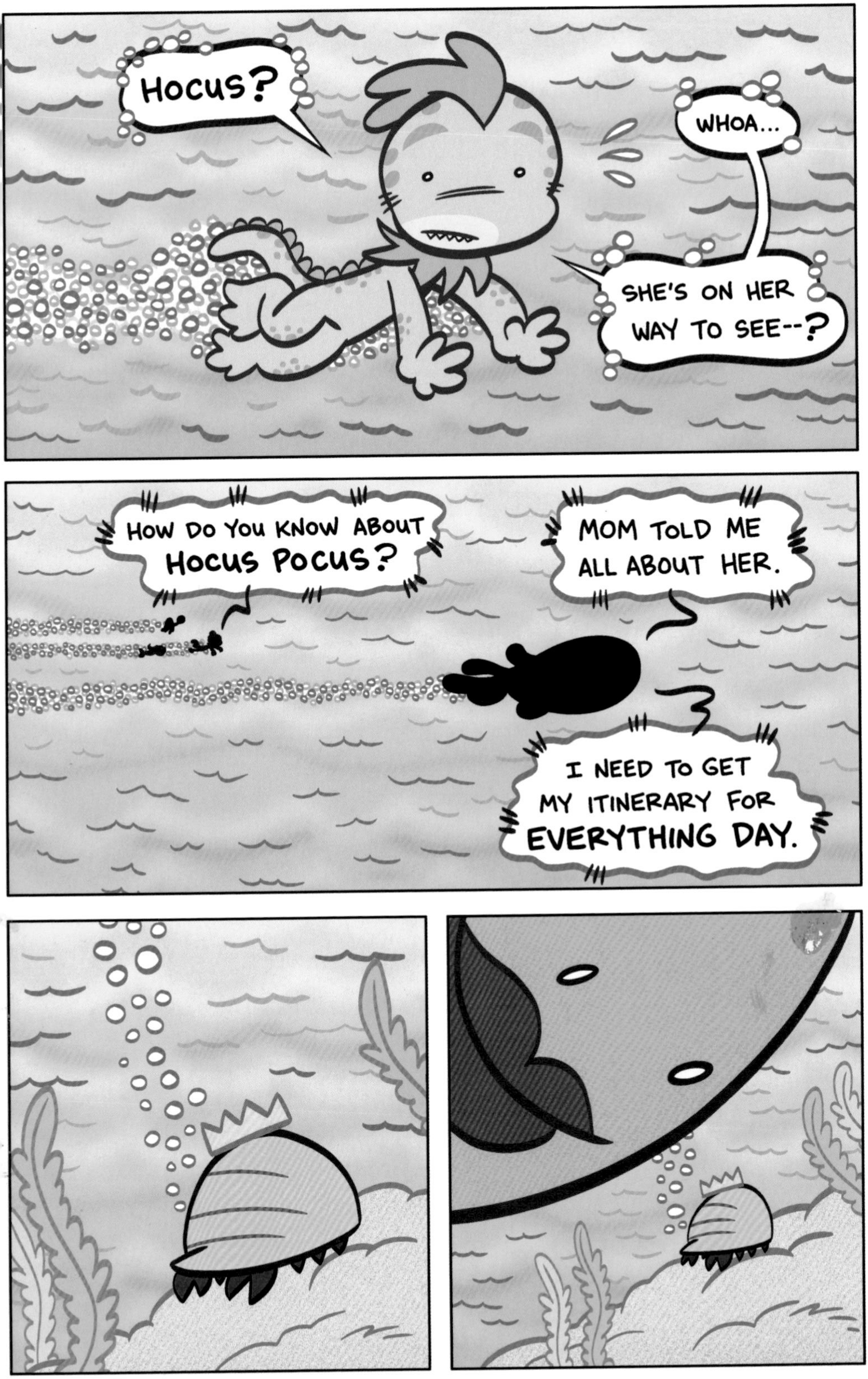
HOCUS?
WHOA...
SHE'S ON HER WAY TO SEE--?
HOW DO YOU KNOW ABOUT HOCUS POCUS?
MOM TOLD ME ALL ABOUT HER.
I NEED TO GET MY ITINERARY FOR EVERYTHING DAY.

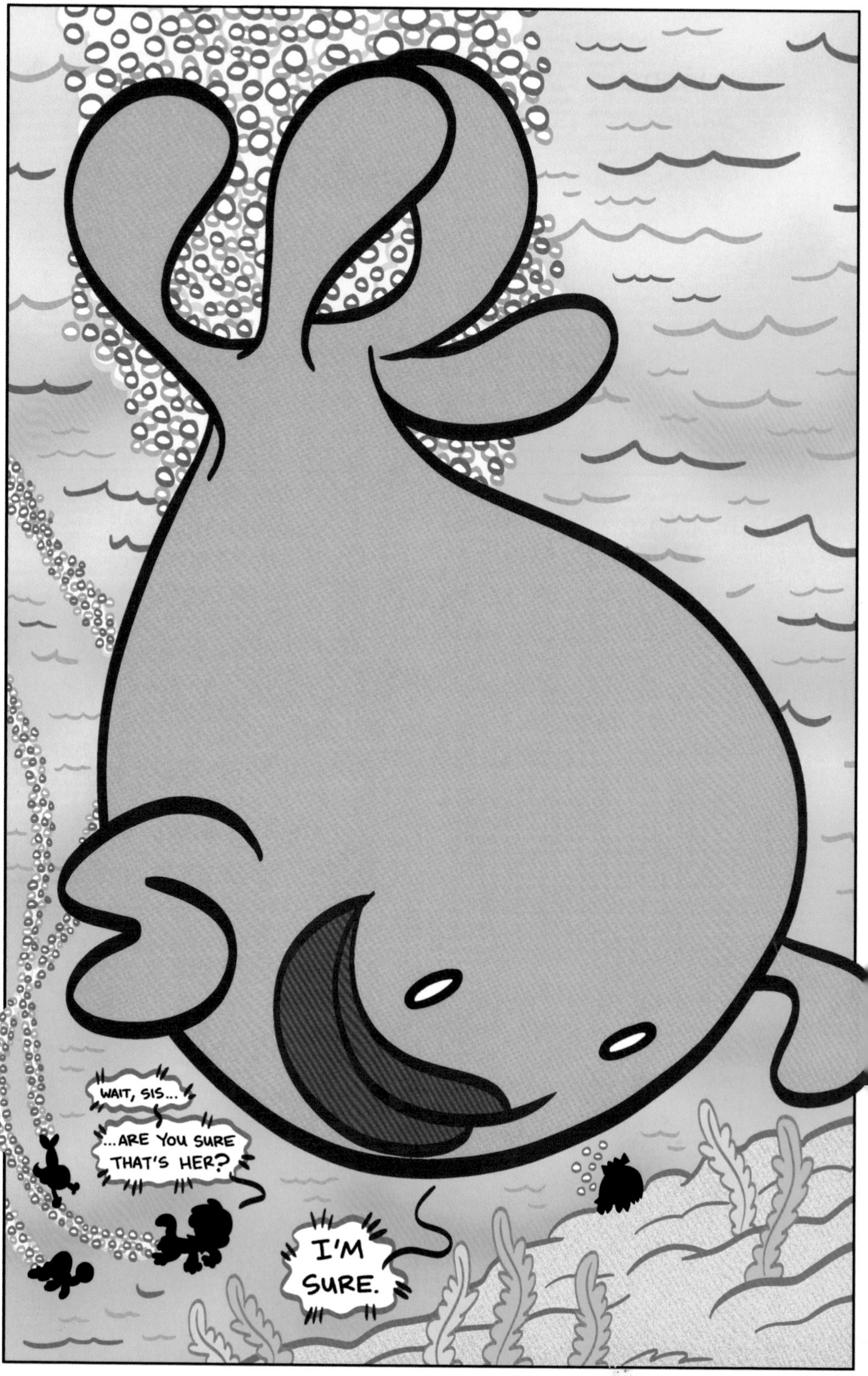
WAIT, SIS...
...ARE YOU SURE THAT'S HER?
I'M SURE.

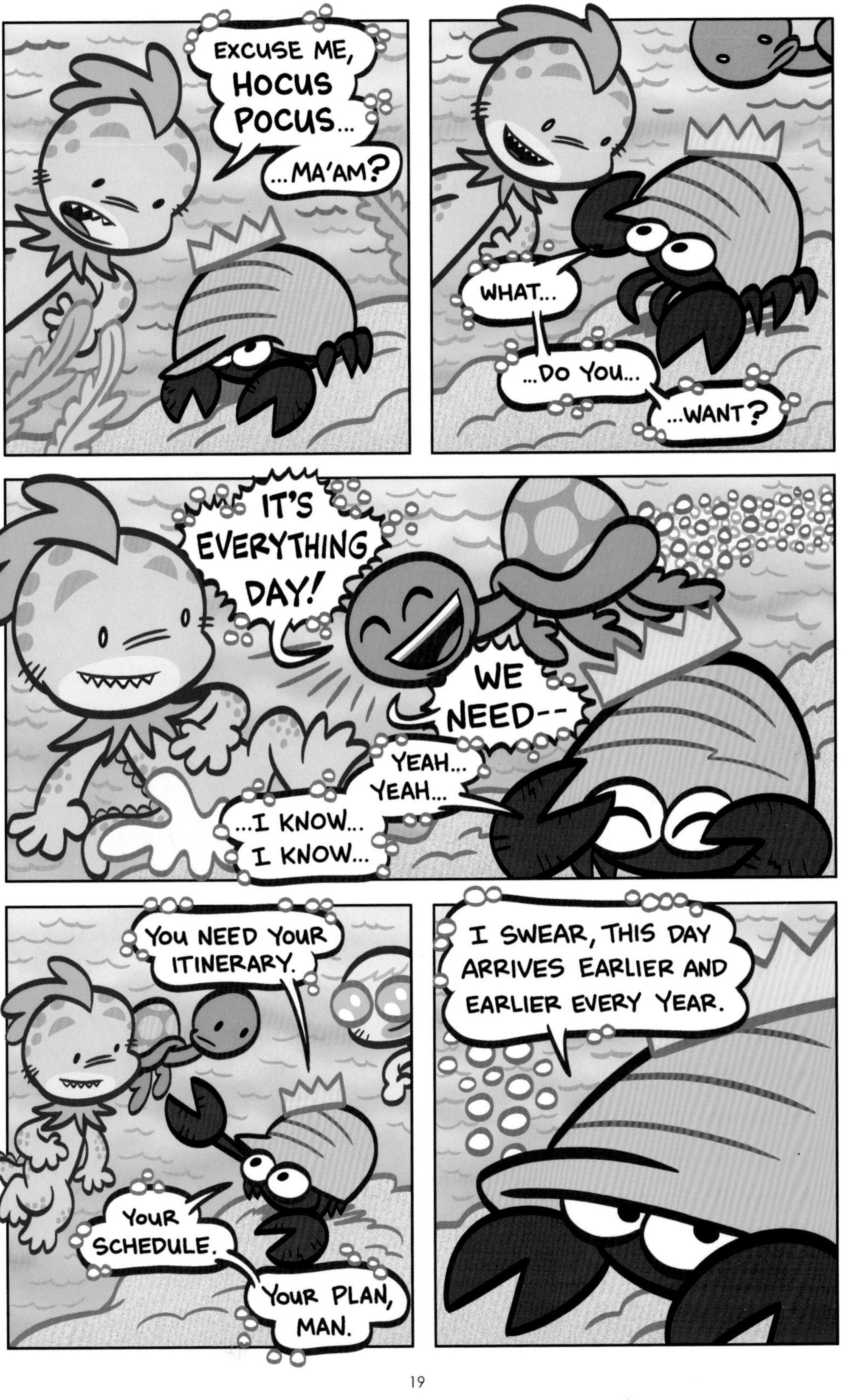
EXCUSE ME, HOCUS POCUS...
...MA'AM?
WHAT...
...DO YOU...
...WANT?
IT'S EVERYTHING DAY!
WE NEED--
YEAH... YEAH...
...I KNOW... I KNOW...
YOU NEED YOUR ITINERARY.
YOUR SCHEDULE.
YOUR PLAN, MAN.
I SWEAR, THIS DAY ARRIVES EARLIER AND EARLIER EVERY YEAR.

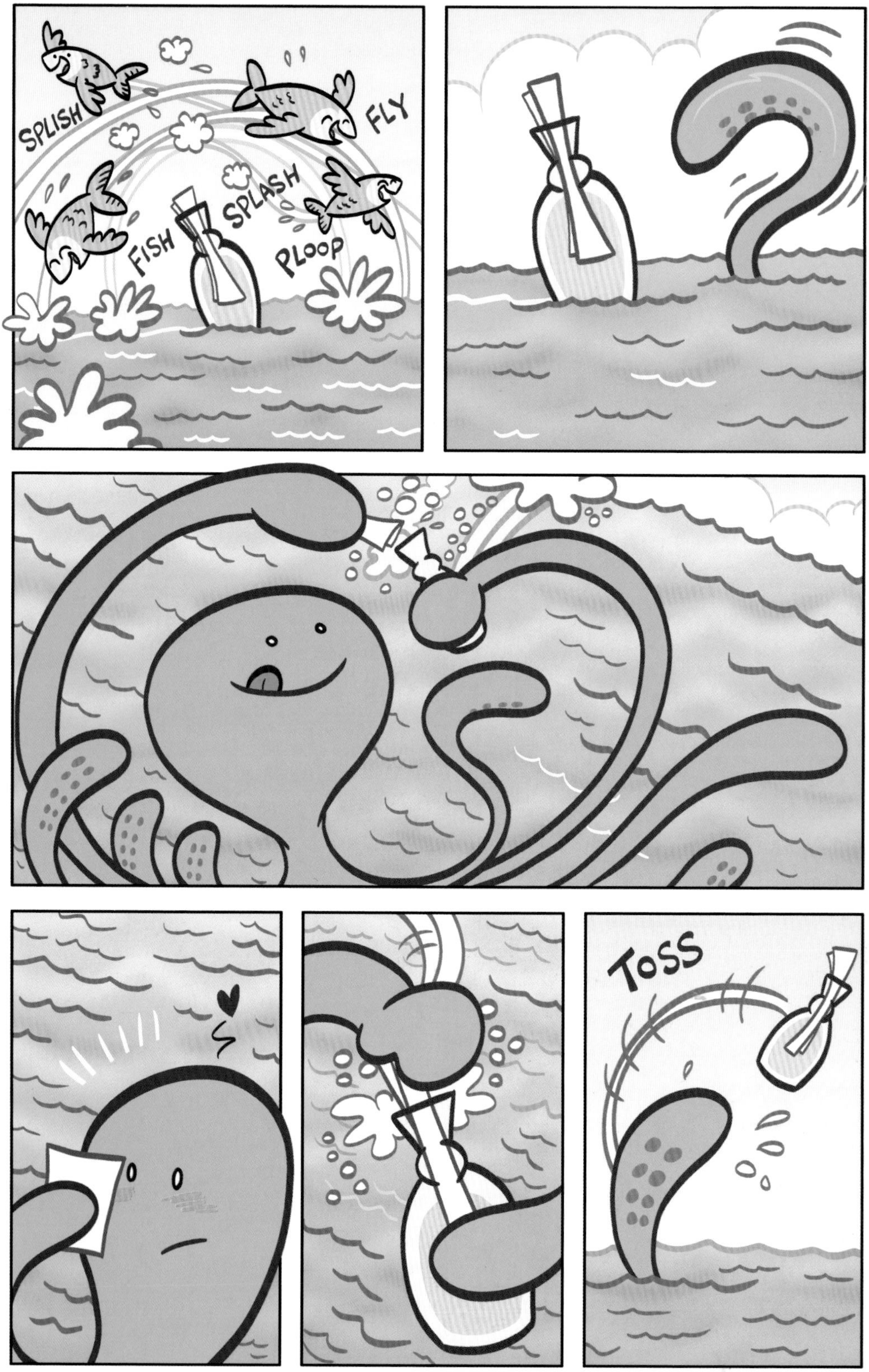
SPLISH
FLY
FISH
SPLASH
PLOOP
TOSS

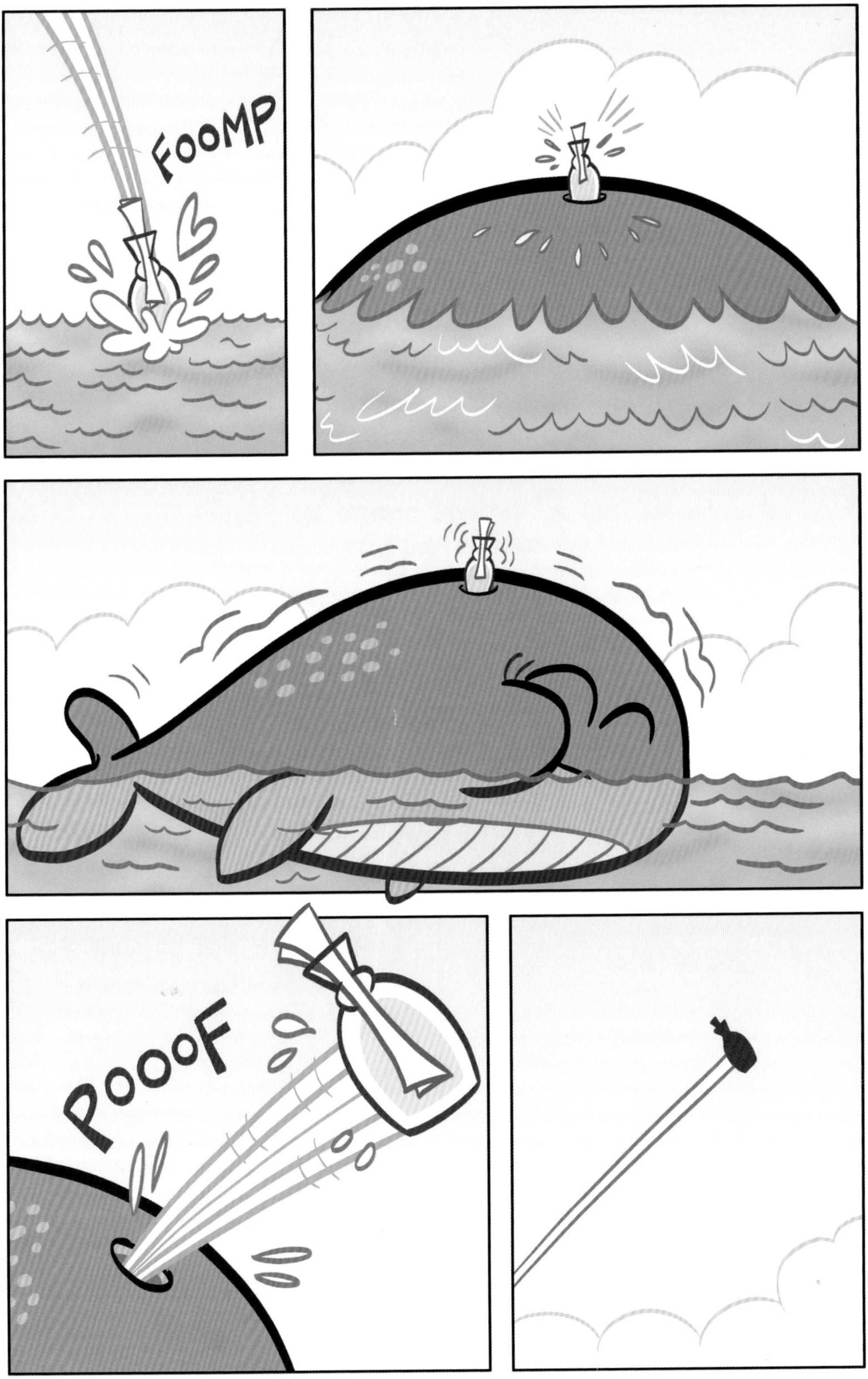
FOOMP
POOOF

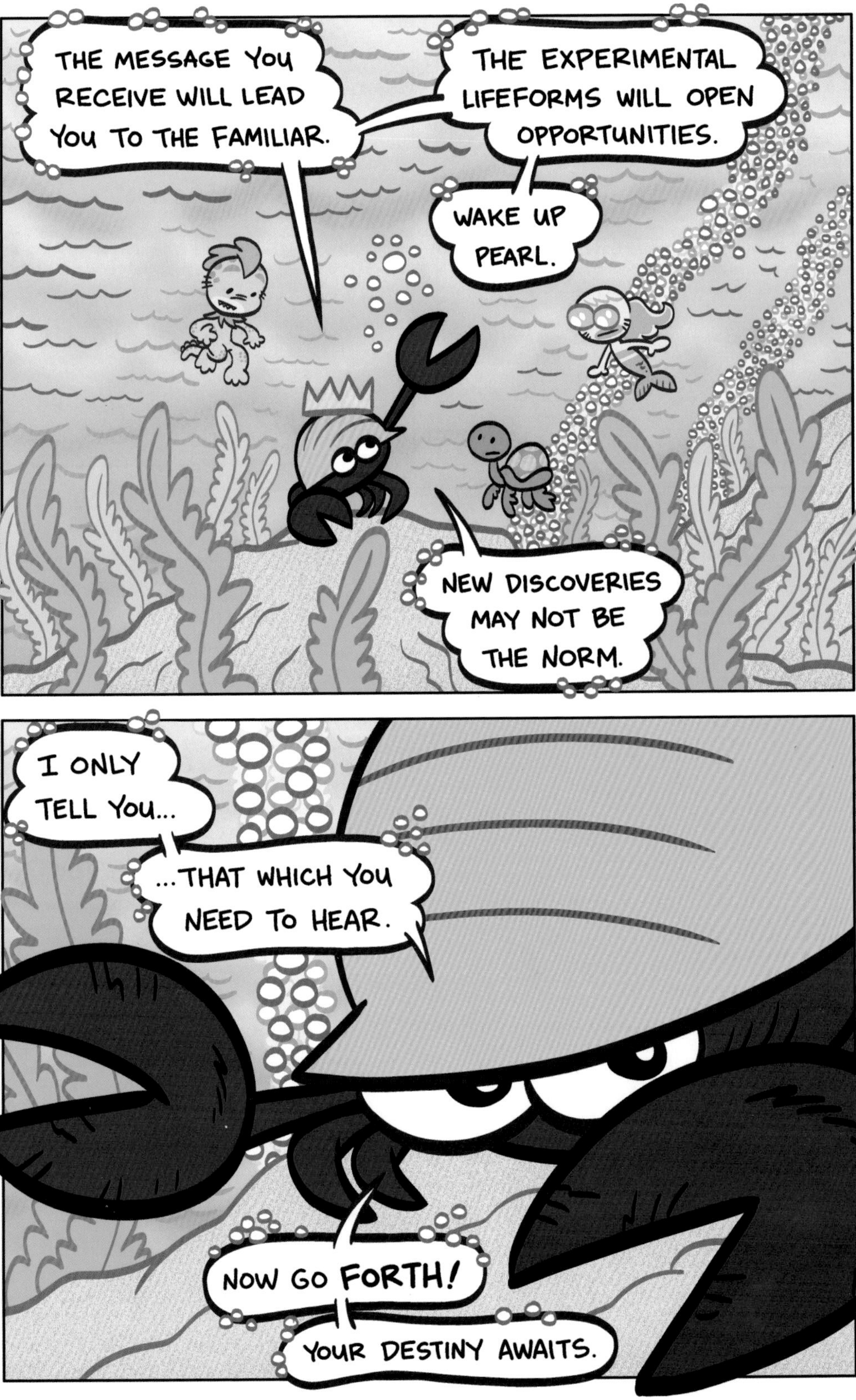
THE MESSAGE YOU RECEIVE WILL LEAD YOU TO THE FAMILIAR.
THE EXPERIMENTAL LIFEFORMS WILL OPEN OPPORTUNITIES.
WAKE UP PEARL.
NEW DISCOVERIES MAY NOT BE THE NORM.
I ONLY TELL YOU...
...THAT WHICH YOU NEED TO HEAR.
NOW GO FORTH!
YOUR DESTINY AWAITS.

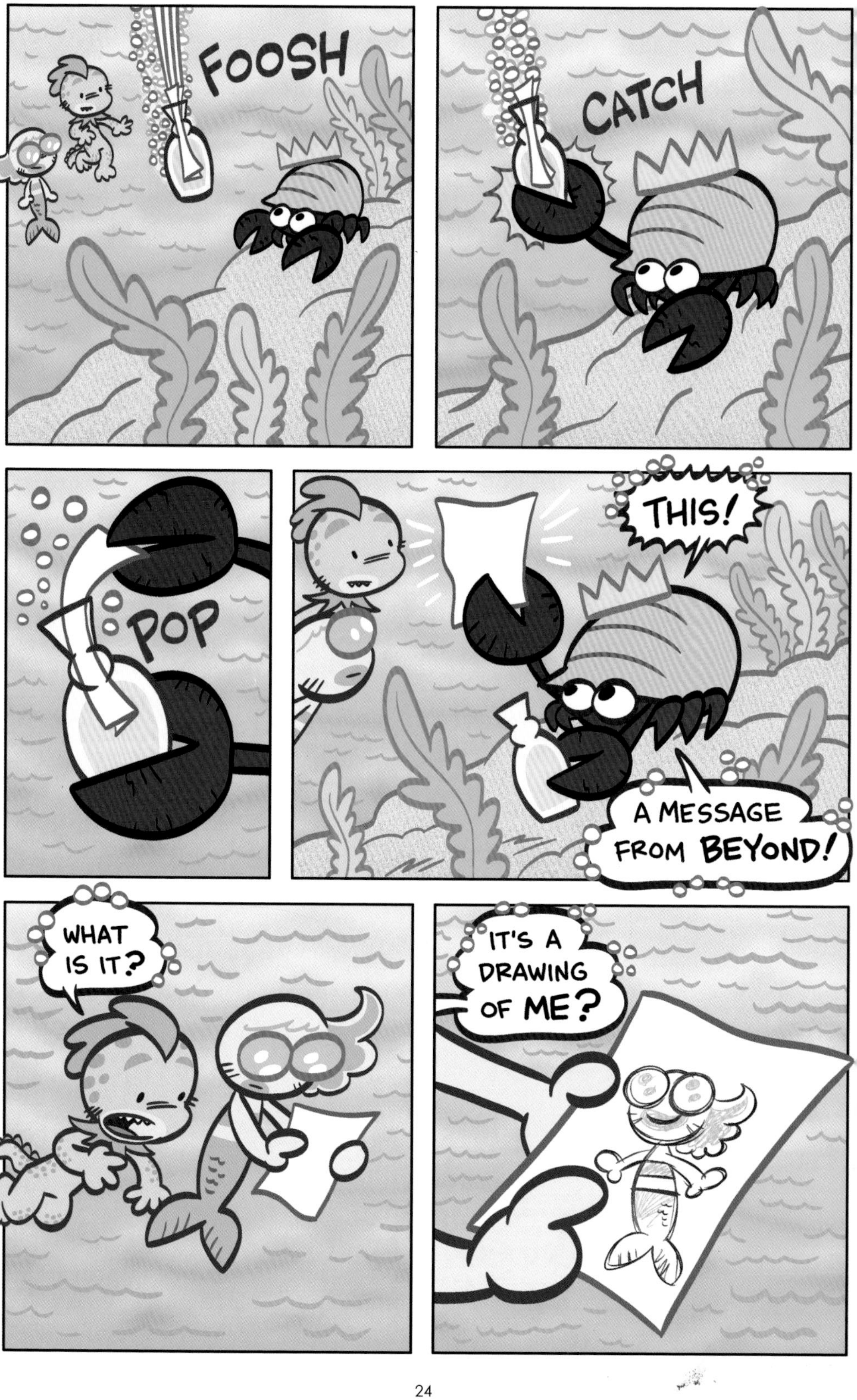
FOOSH
CATCH
POP
THIS!
A MESSAGE FROM BEYOND!
WHAT IS IT?
IT'S A DRAWING OF ME?

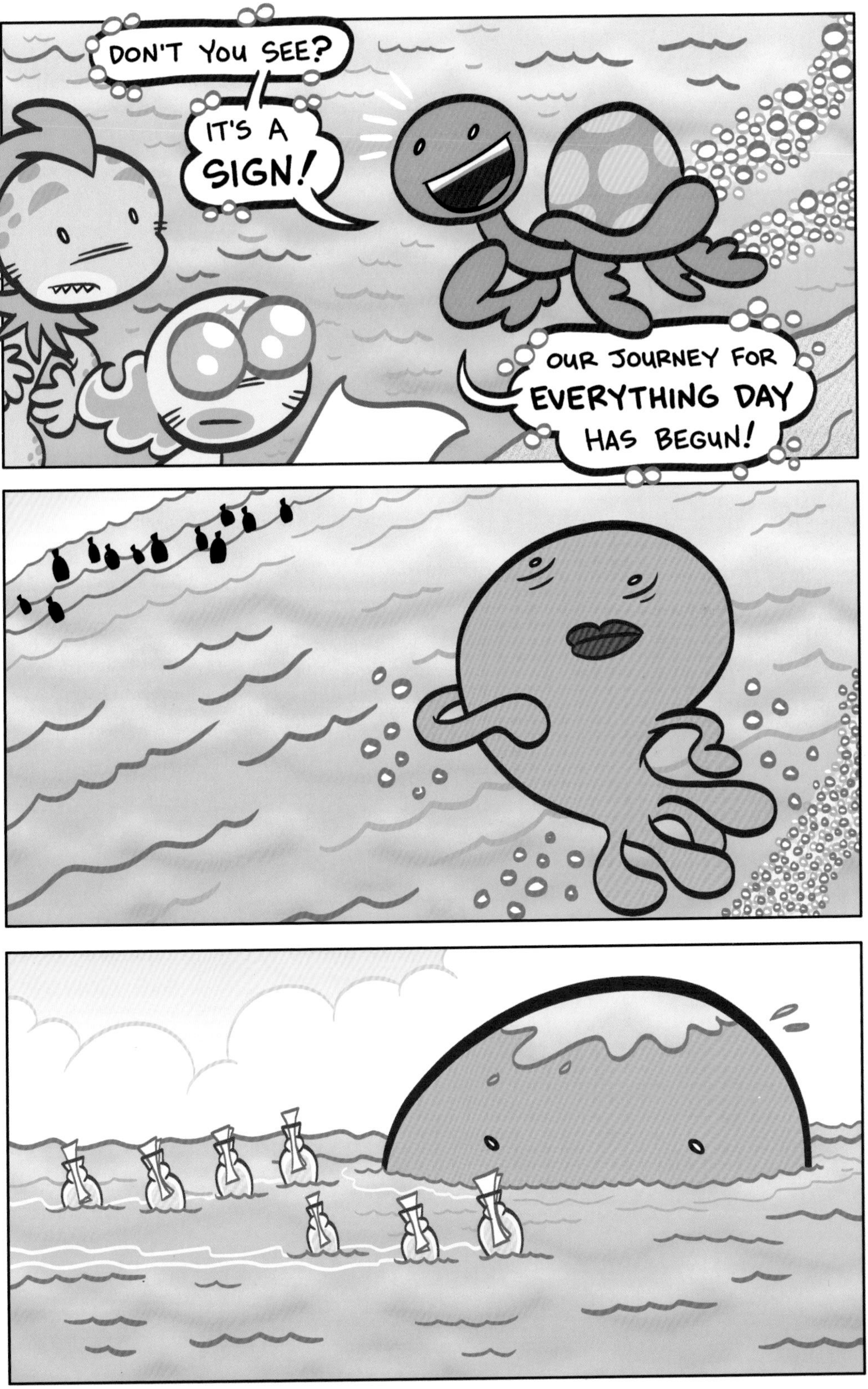
DON'T YOU SEE?
IT'S A SIGN!
OUR JOURNEY FOR EVERYTHING DAY HAS BEGUN!

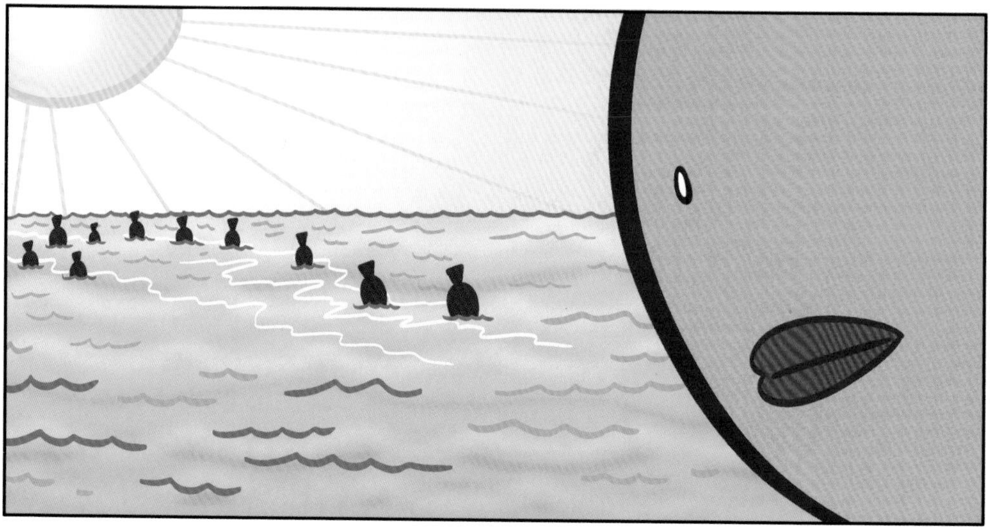

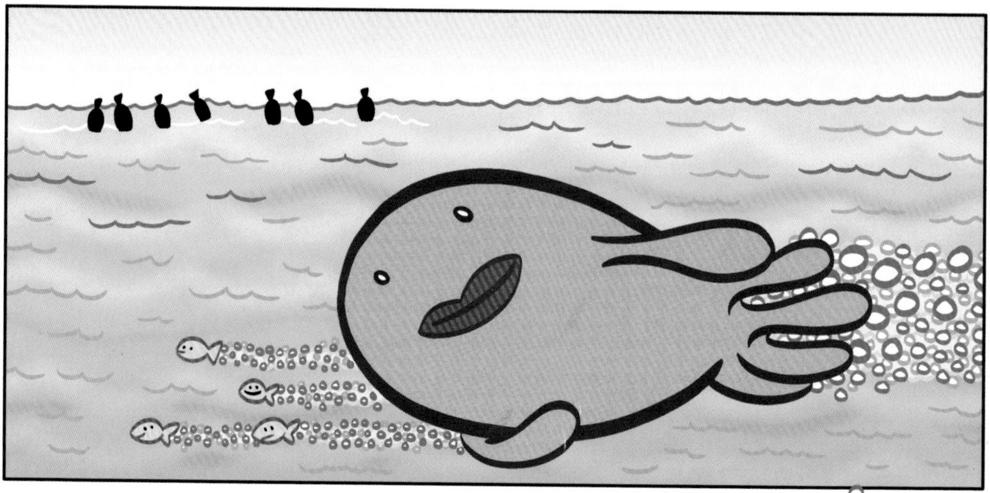

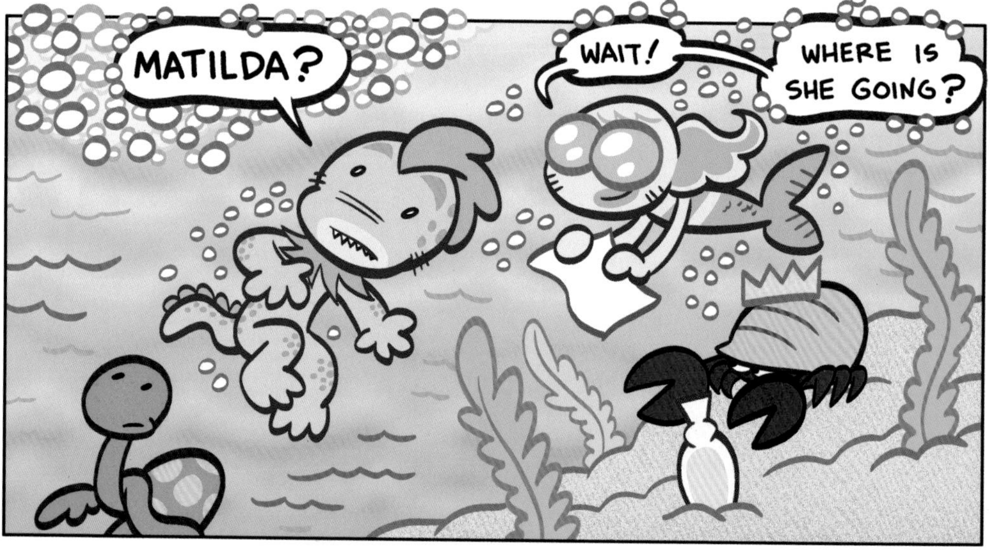
MATILDA?
WAIT!
WHERE IS SHE GOING?

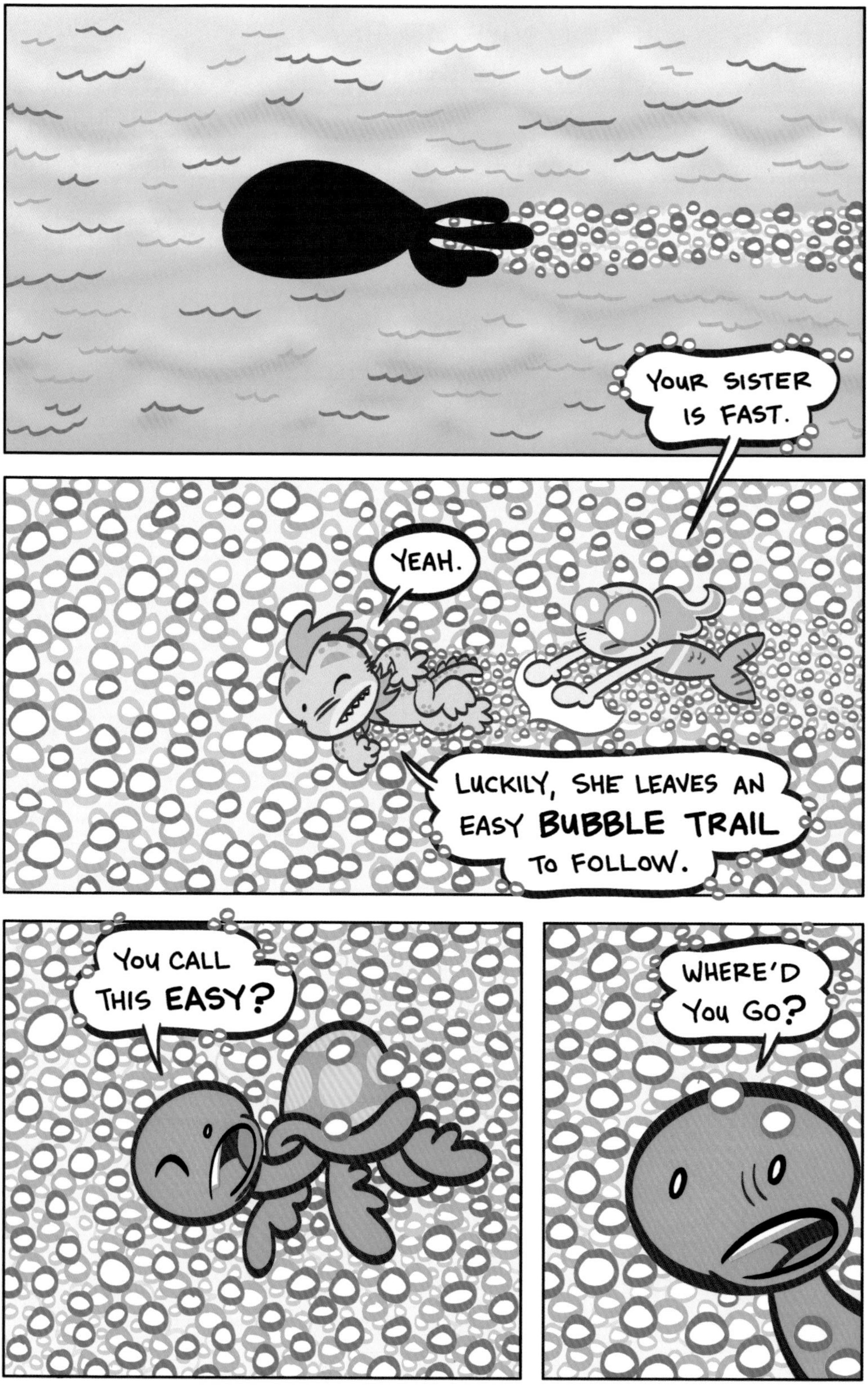
YOUR SISTER IS FAST.
YEAH.
LUCKILY, SHE LEAVES AN EASY BUBBLE TRAIL TO FOLLOW.
YOU CALL THIS EASY?
WHERE'D YOU GO?

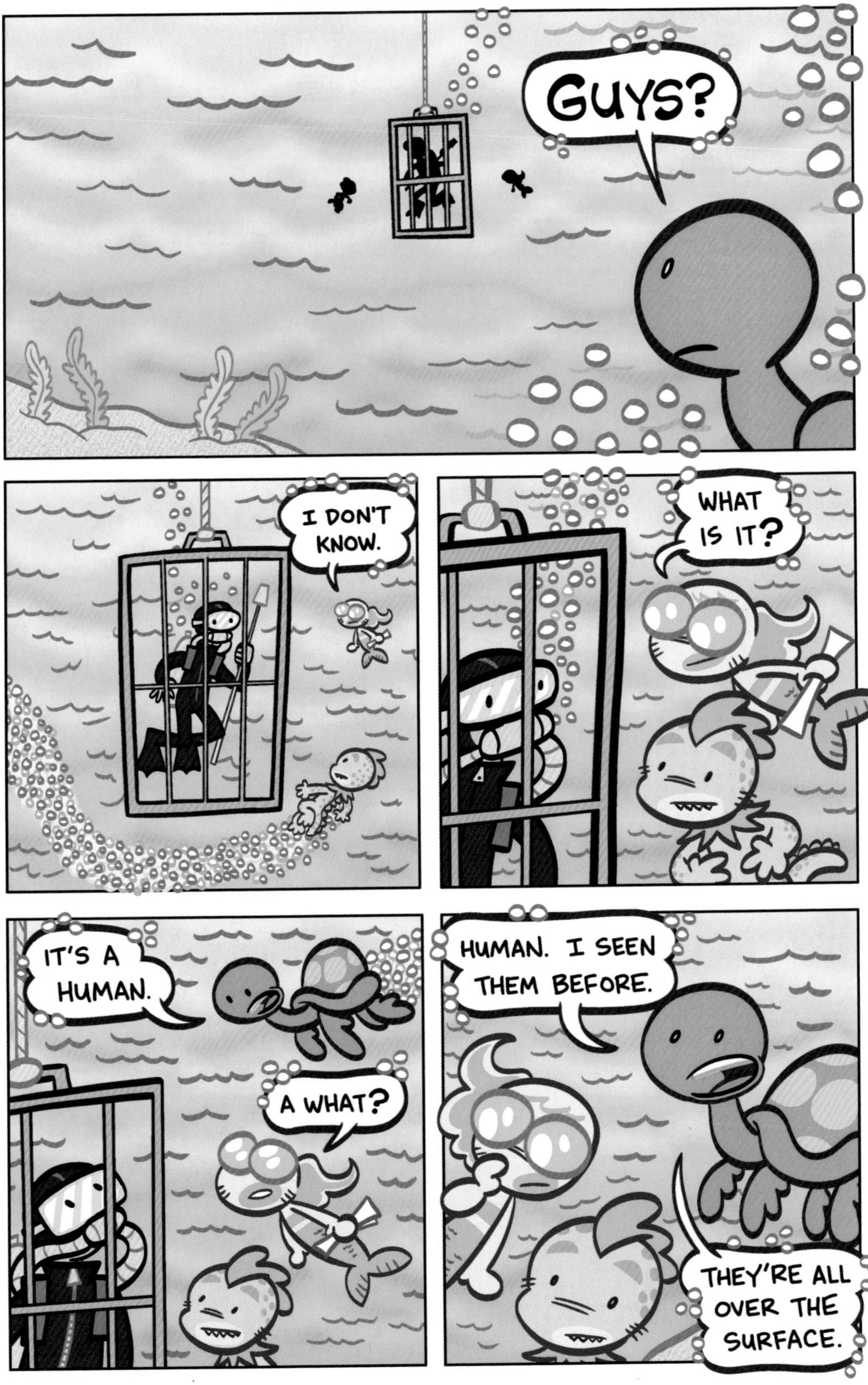
GUYS?
I DON'T KNOW.
WHAT IS IT?
IT'S A HUMAN.
A WHAT?
HUMAN. I SEEN THEM BEFORE.
THEY'RE ALL OVER THE SURFACE.

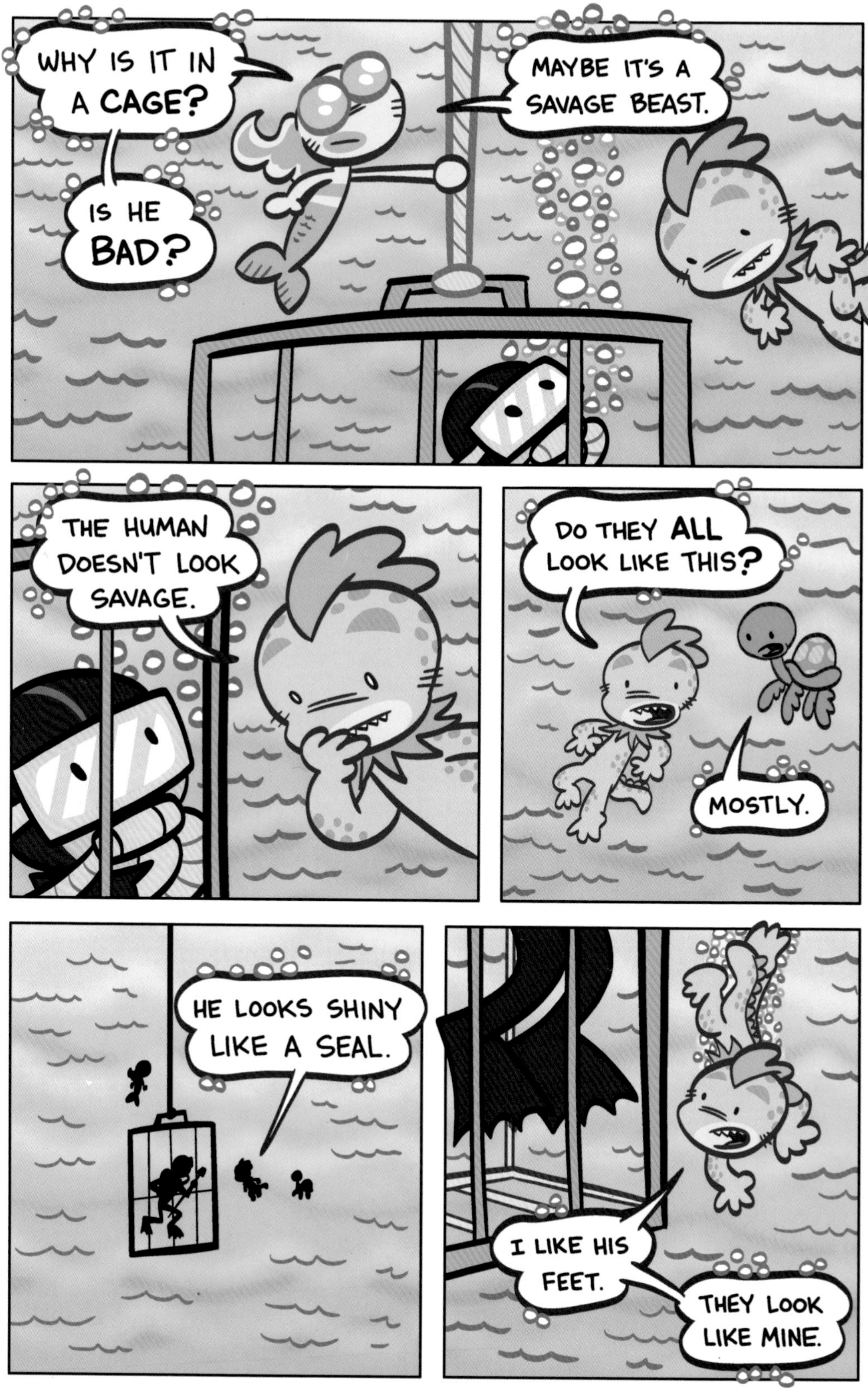

WHY IS IT IN A CAGE?
IS HE BAD?
MAYBE IT'S A SAVAGE BEAST.
THE HUMAN DOESN'T LOOK SAVAGE.
DO THEY ALL LOOK LIKE THIS?
MOSTLY.
HE LOOKS SHINY LIKE A SEAL.
I LIKE HIS FEET.
THEY LOOK LIKE MINE.

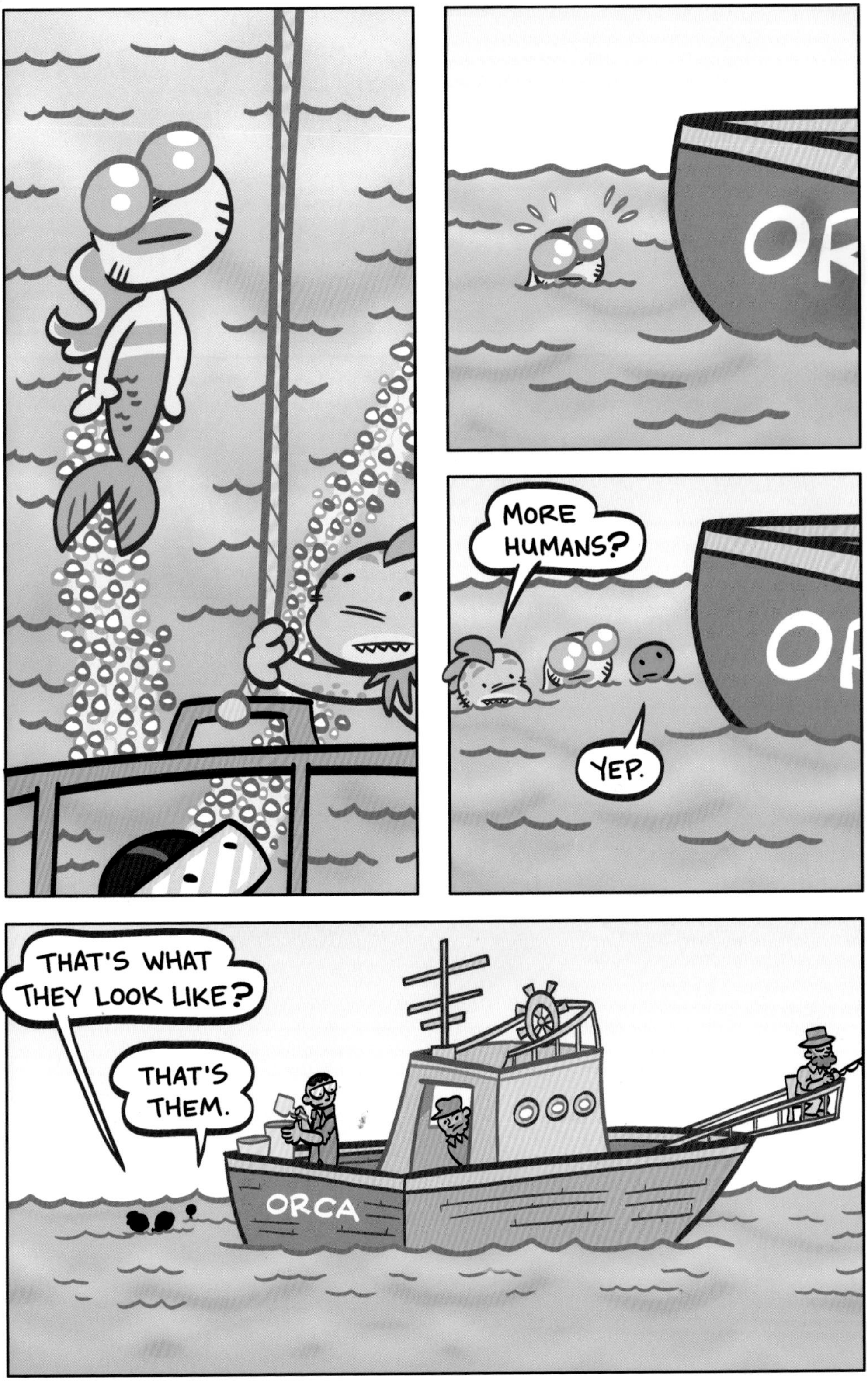
MORE HUMANS?
YEP.
ORCA
THAT'S WHAT THEY LOOK LIKE?
THAT'S THEM.

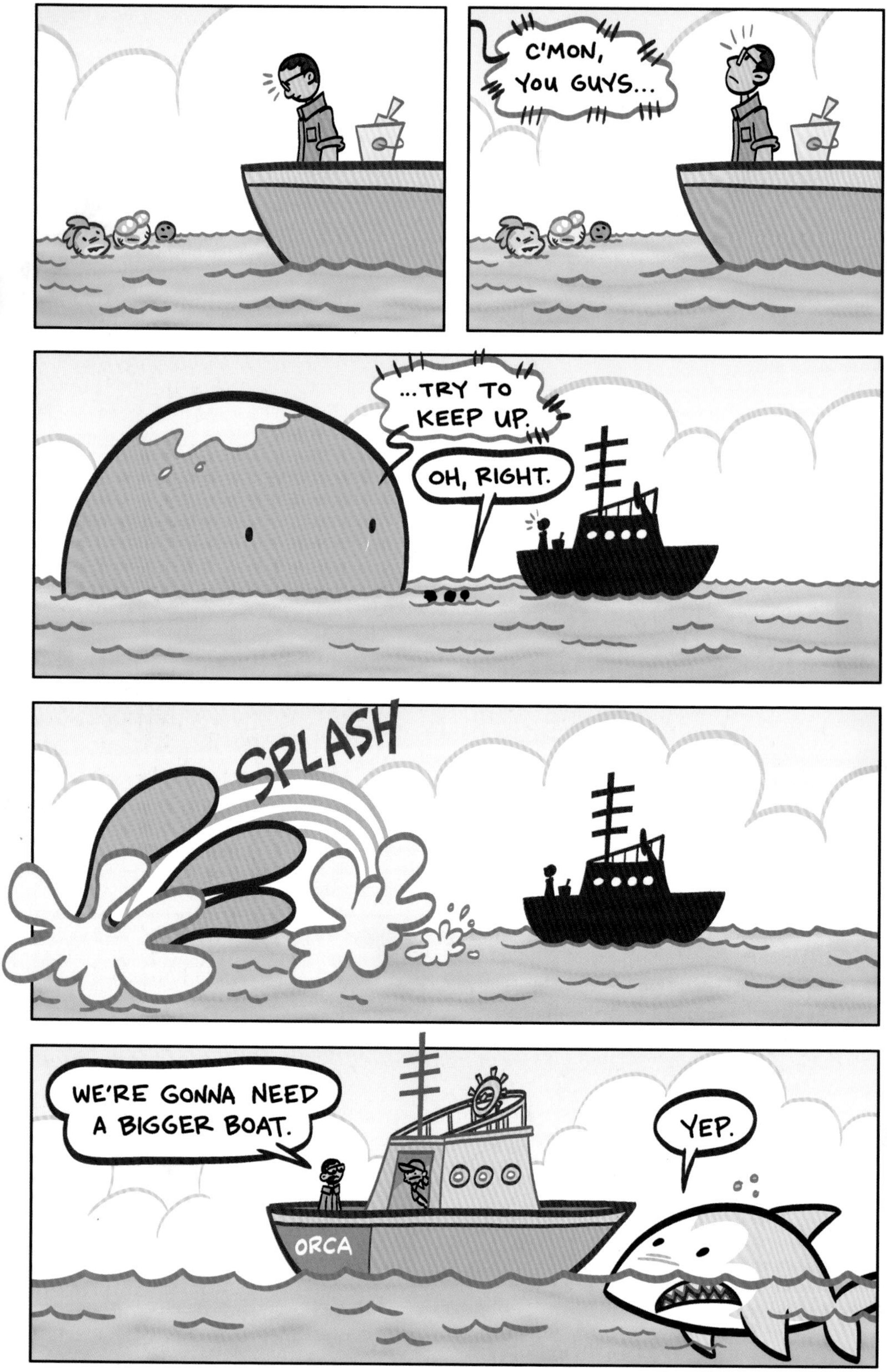
C'MON, YOU GUYS...
...TRY TO KEEP UP.
OH, RIGHT.
SPLASH
WE'RE GONNA NEED A BIGGER BOAT.
YEP.
ORCA

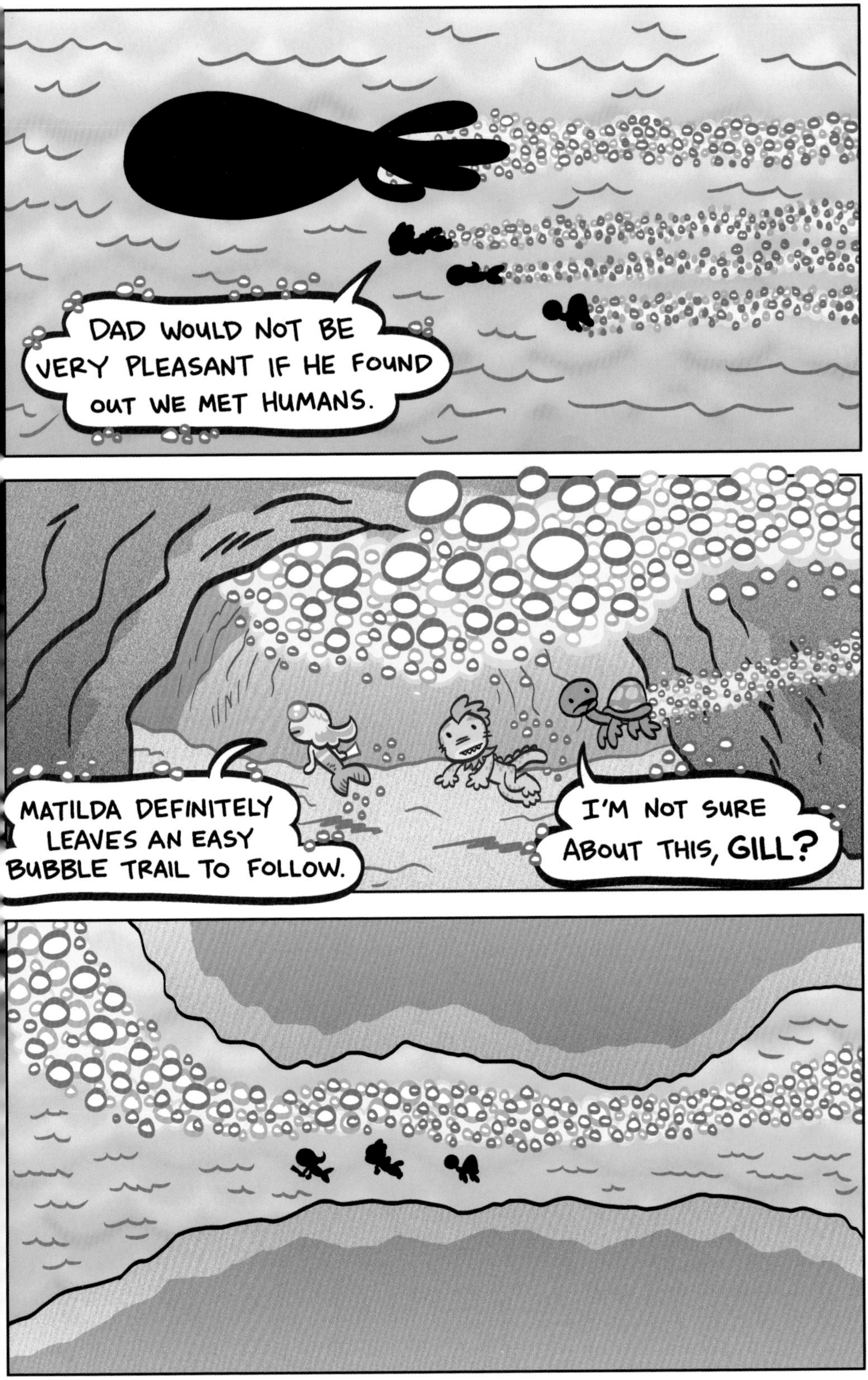
DAD WOULD NOT BE VERY PLEASANT IF HE FOUND OUT WE MET HUMANS.
MATILDA DEFINITELY LEAVES AN EASY BUBBLE TRAIL TO FOLLOW.
I'M NOT SURE ABOUT THIS, GILL?

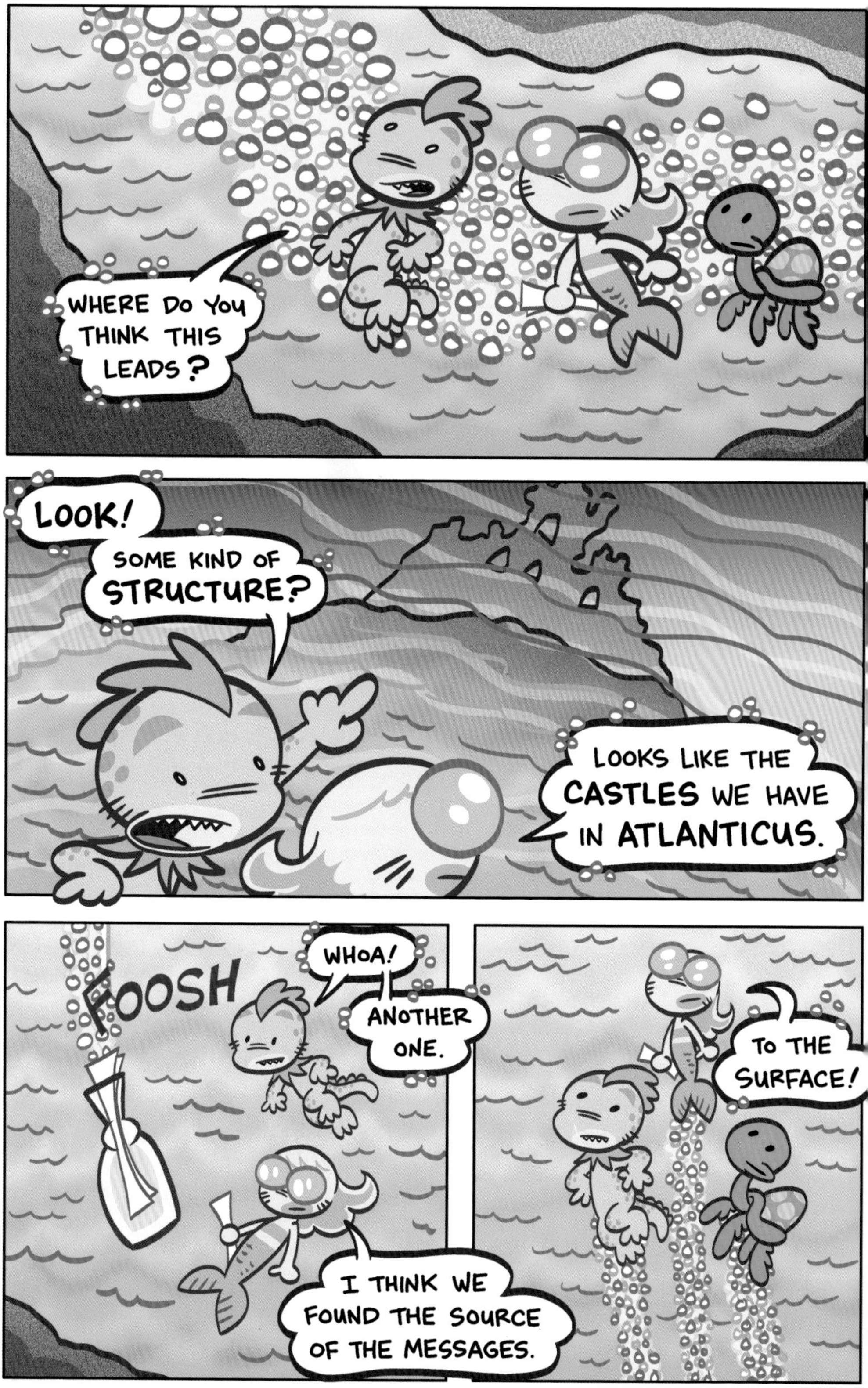
WHERE DO YOU THINK THIS LEADS?
LOOK!
SOME KIND OF STRUCTURE?
LOOKS LIKE THE CASTLES WE HAVE IN ATLANTICUS.
FOOSH
WHOA!
ANOTHER ONE.
I THINK WE FOUND THE SOURCE OF THE MESSAGES.
TO THE SURFACE!

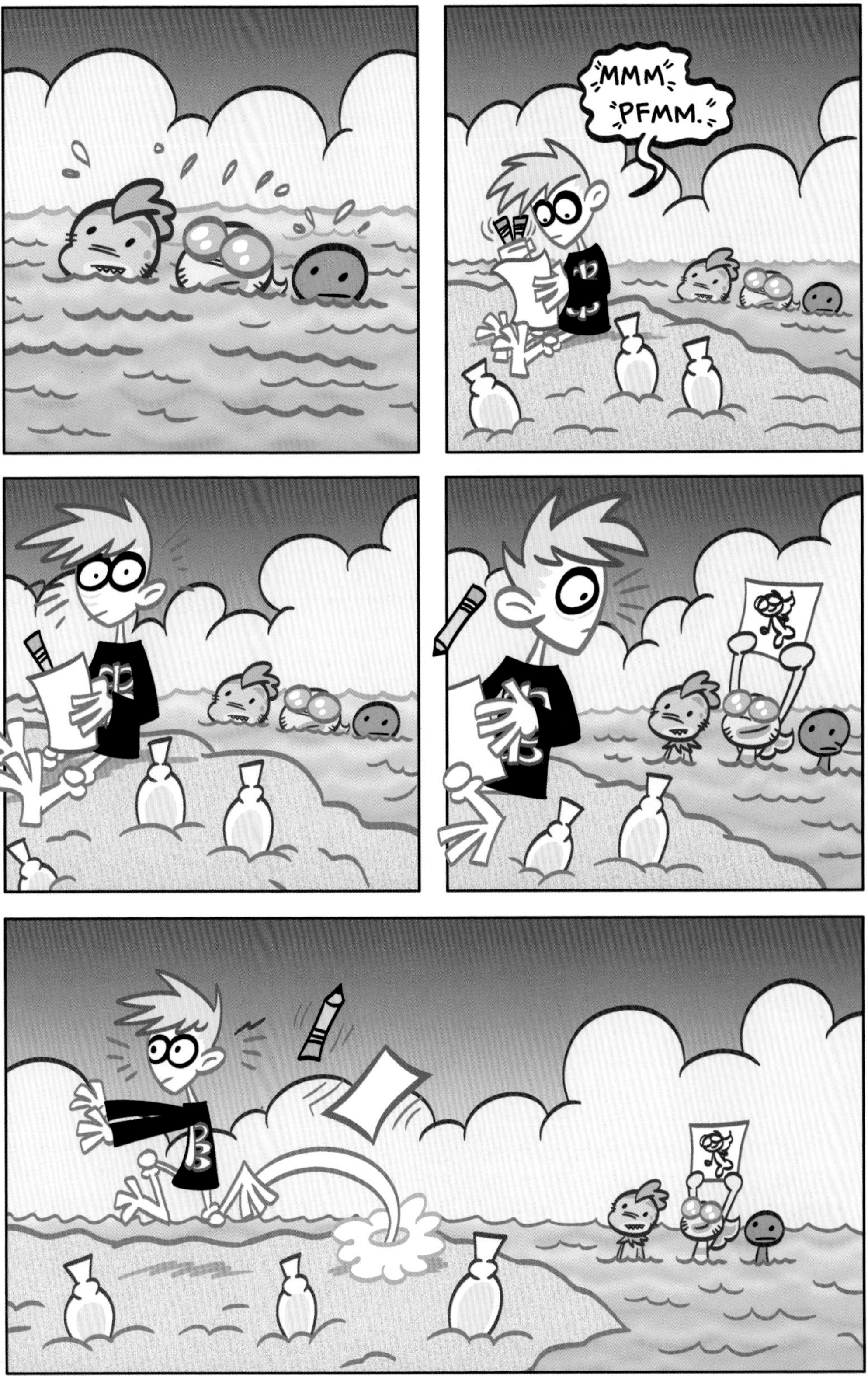
MMM. PFMM.

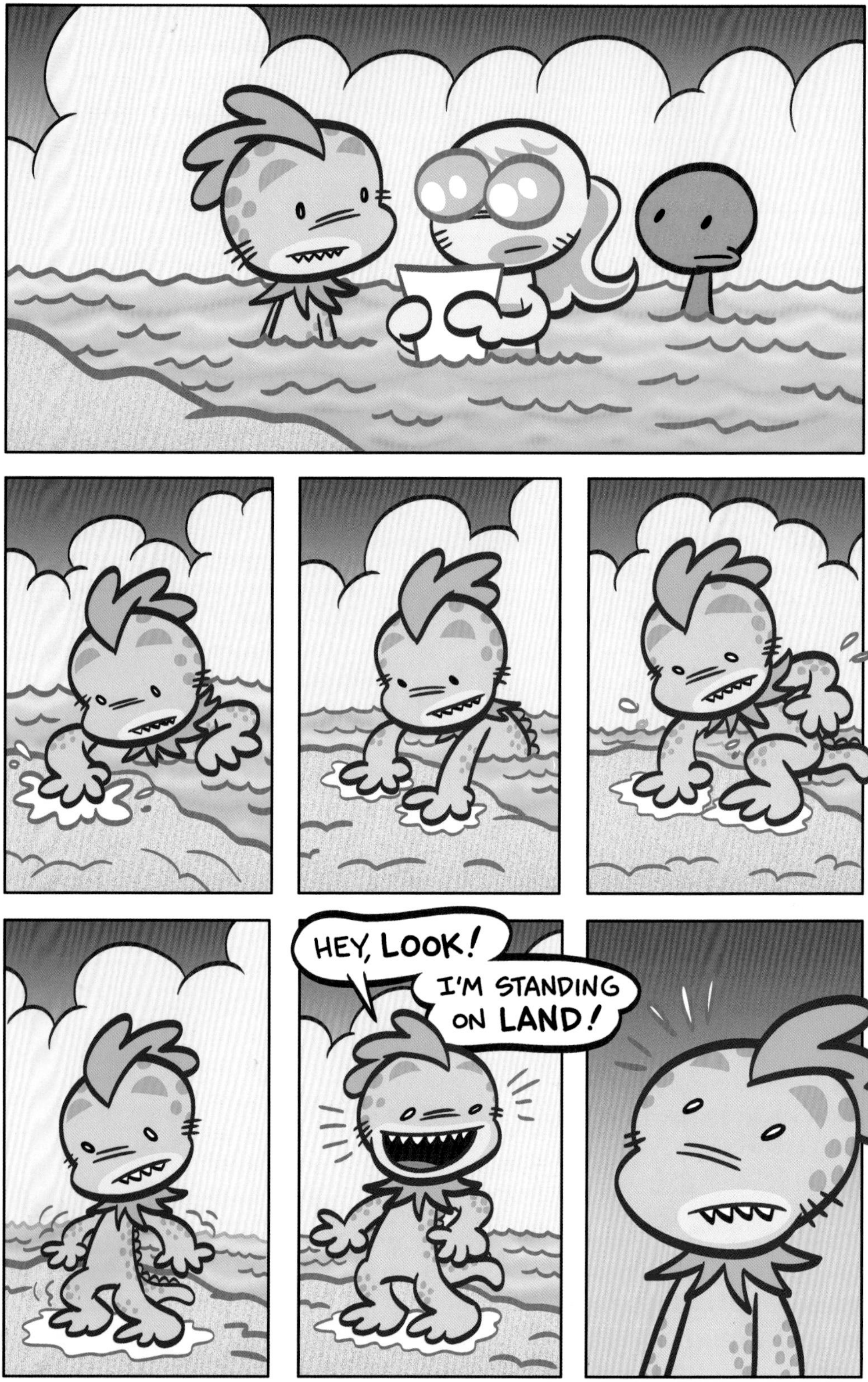
HEY, LOOK!
I'M STANDING ON LAND!

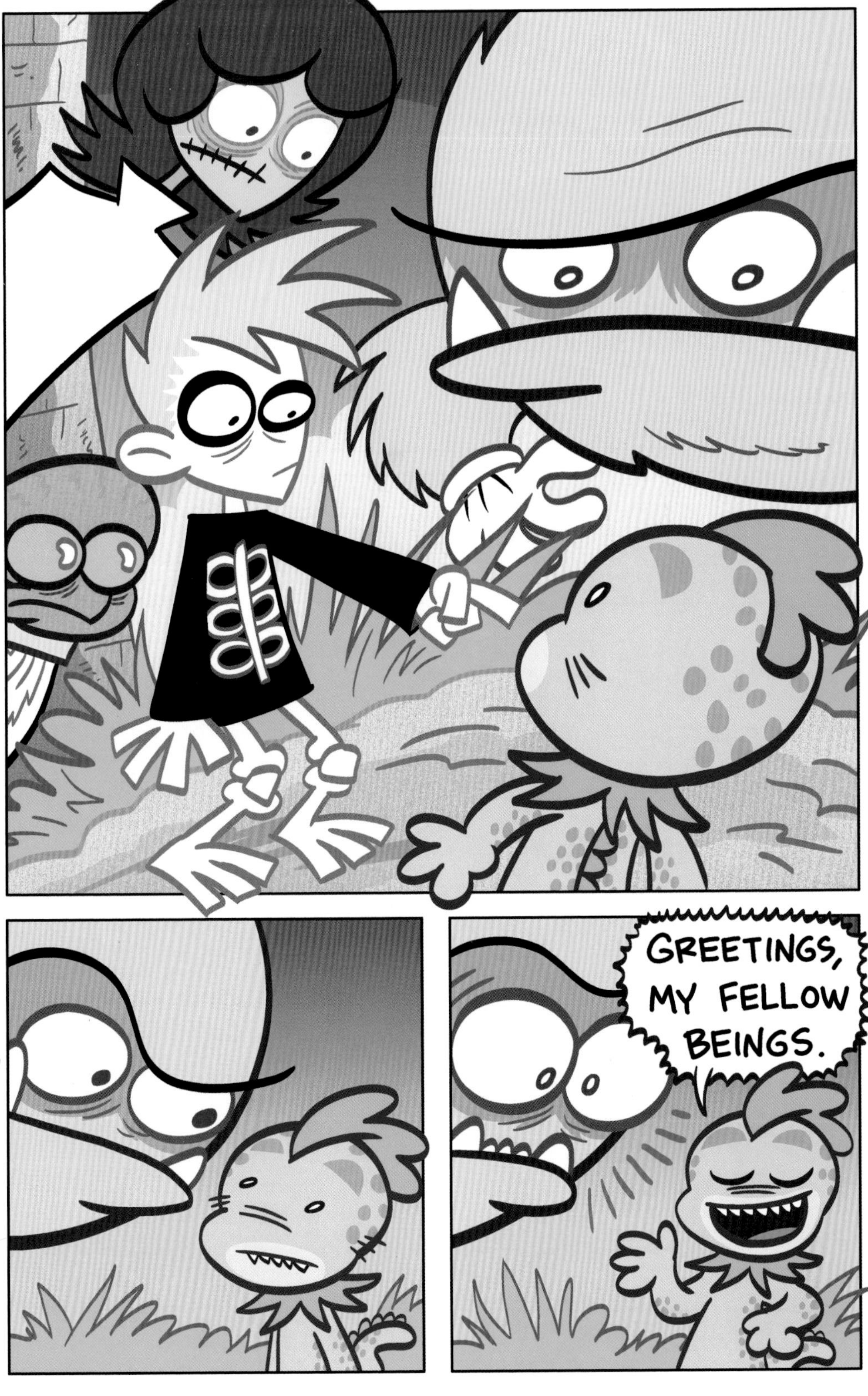
GREETINGS, MY FELLOW BEINGS.

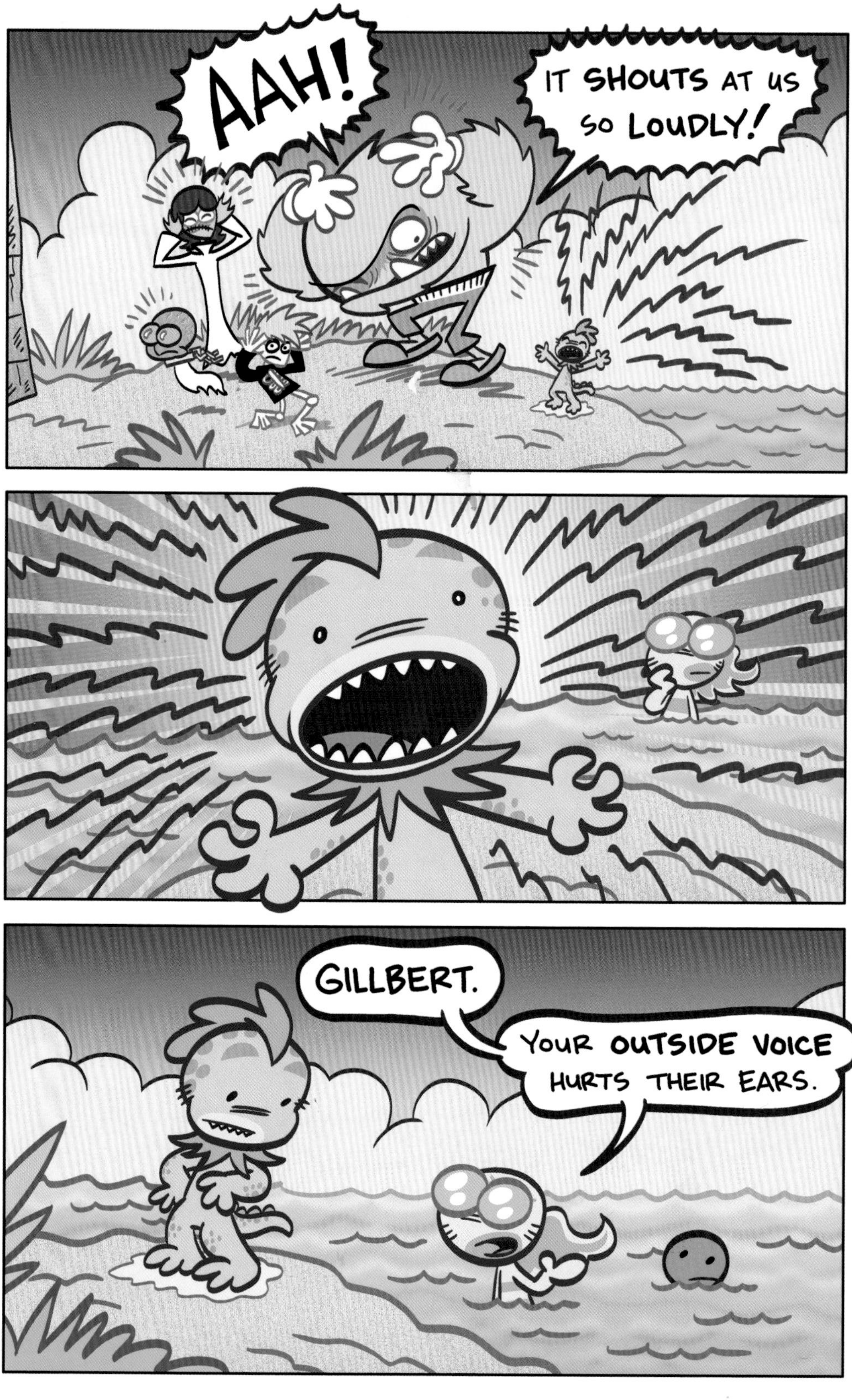
AAH!
IT SHOUTS AT US SO LOUDLY!
GILLBERT.
YOUR OUTSIDE VOICE HURTS THEIR EARS.

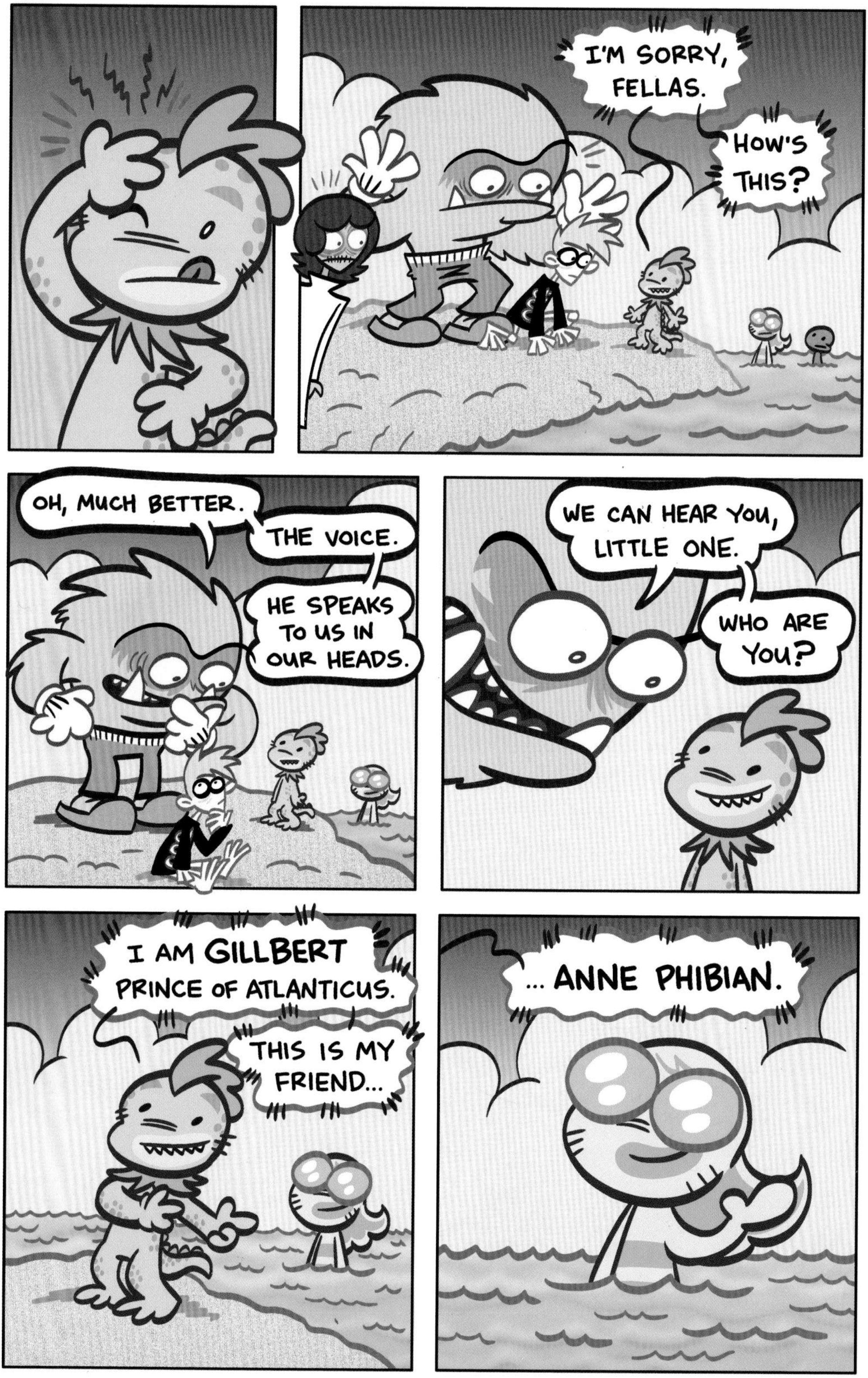
I'M SORRY, FELLAS.
HOW'S THIS?
OH, MUCH BETTER.
THE VOICE.
HE SPEAKS TO US IN OUR HEADS.
WE CAN HEAR YOU, LITTLE ONE.
WHO ARE YOU?
I AM GILLBERT PRINCE OF ATLANTICUS.
THIS IS MY FRIEND...
... ANNE PHIBIAN.

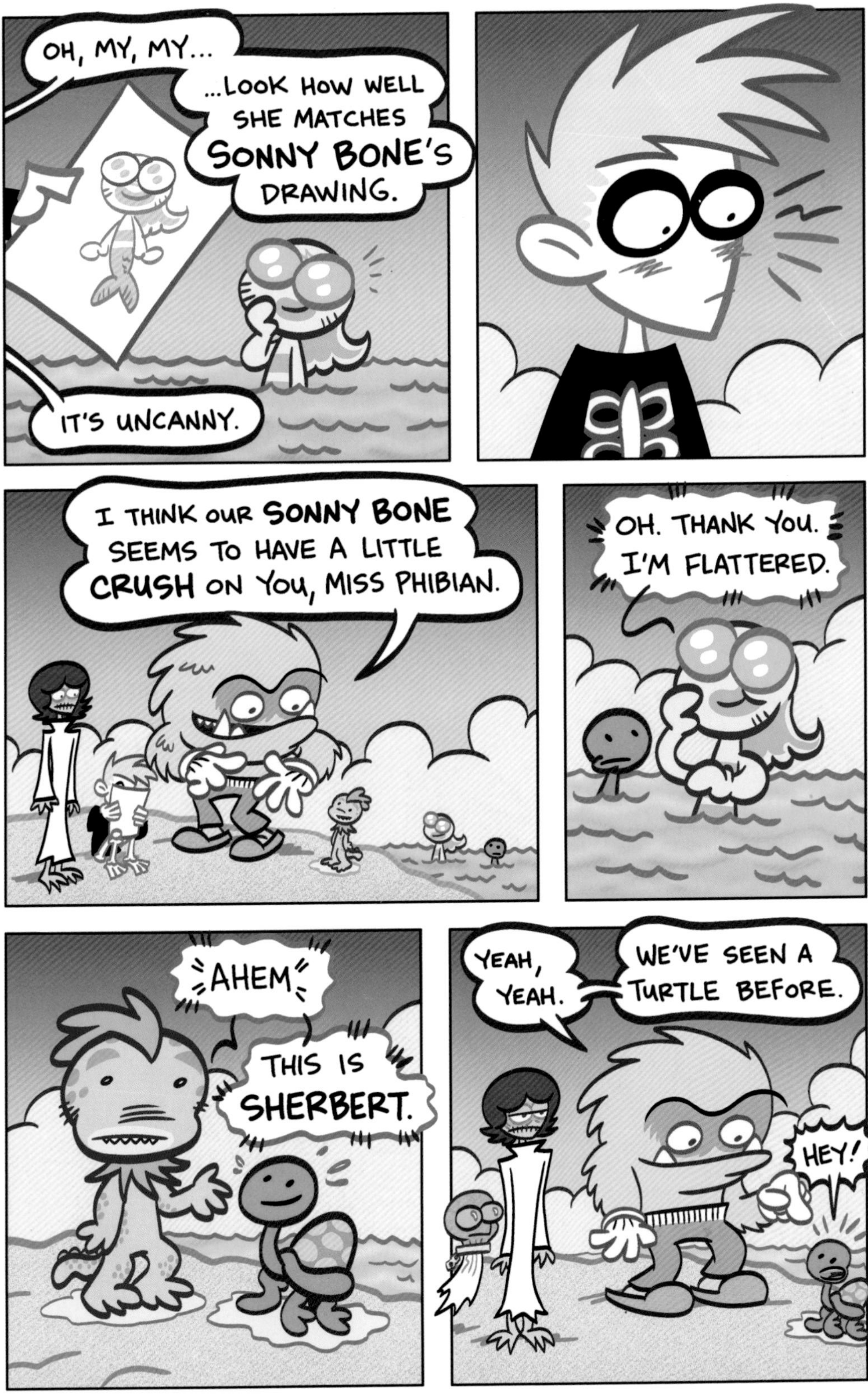
OH, MY, MY...
...LOOK HOW WELL SHE MATCHES SONNY BONE'S DRAWING.
IT'S UNCANNY.
I THINK OUR SONNY BONE SEEMS TO HAVE A LITTLE CRUSH ON YOU, MISS PHIBIAN.
OH. THANK YOU. I'M FLATTERED.
AHEM
THIS IS SHERBERT.
YEAH, YEAH.
WE'VE SEEN A TURTLE BEFORE.
HEY!

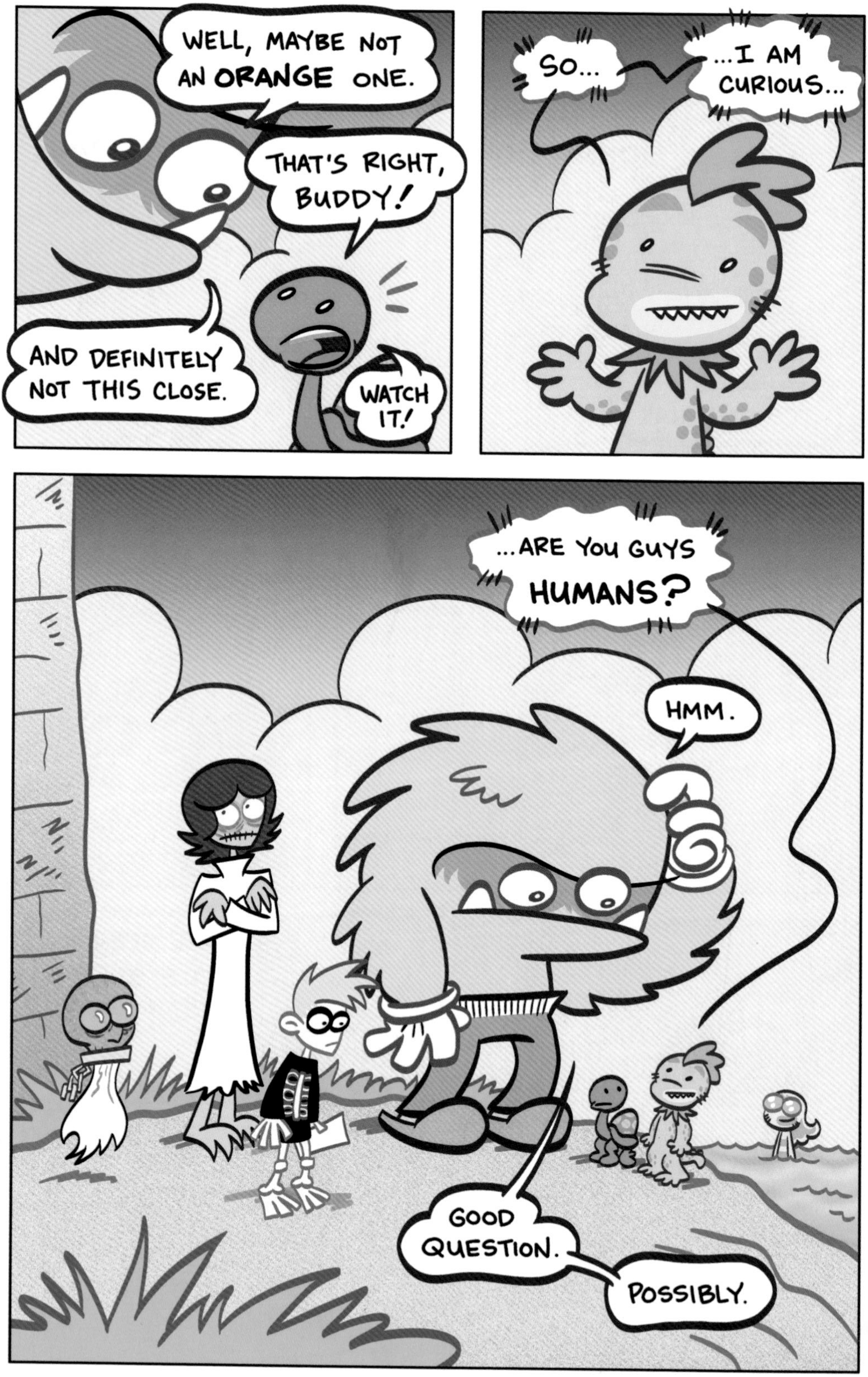
WELL, MAYBE NOT AN ORANGE ONE.
THAT'S RIGHT, BUDDY!
AND DEFINITELY NOT THIS CLOSE.
WATCH IT!
SO...
...I AM CURIOUS...
...ARE YOU GUYS HUMANS?
HMM.
GOOD QUESTION.
POSSIBLY.

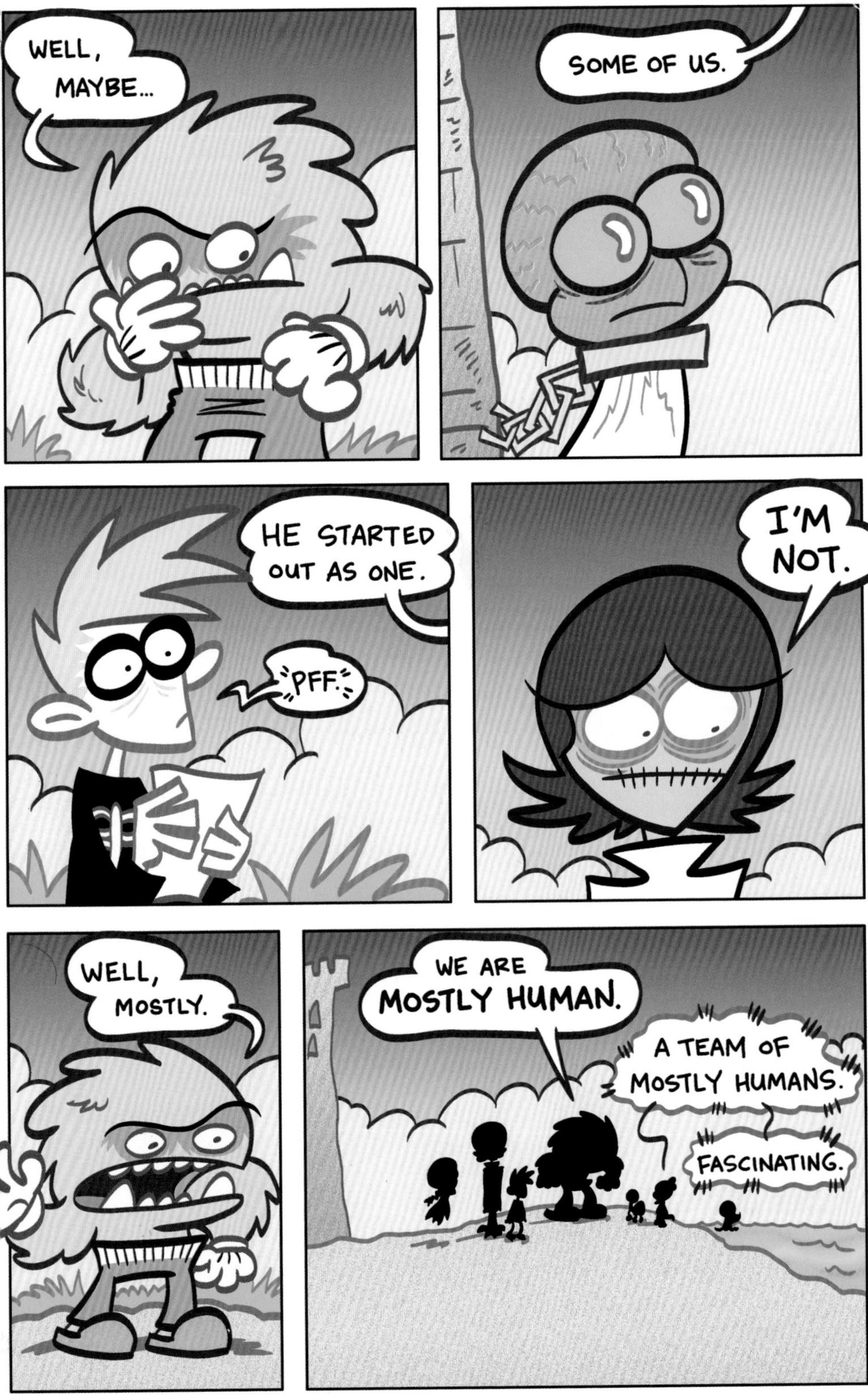

WELL, MAYBE...
SOME OF US.
HE STARTED OUT AS ONE.
PFF.
I'M NOT.
WELL, MOSTLY.
WE ARE MOSTLY HUMAN.
A TEAM OF MOSTLY HUMANS.
FASCINATING.

45

47

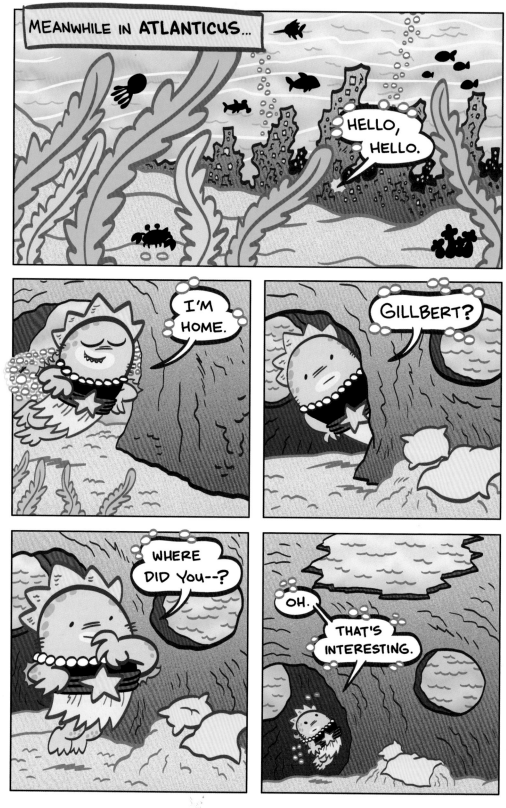

49

53

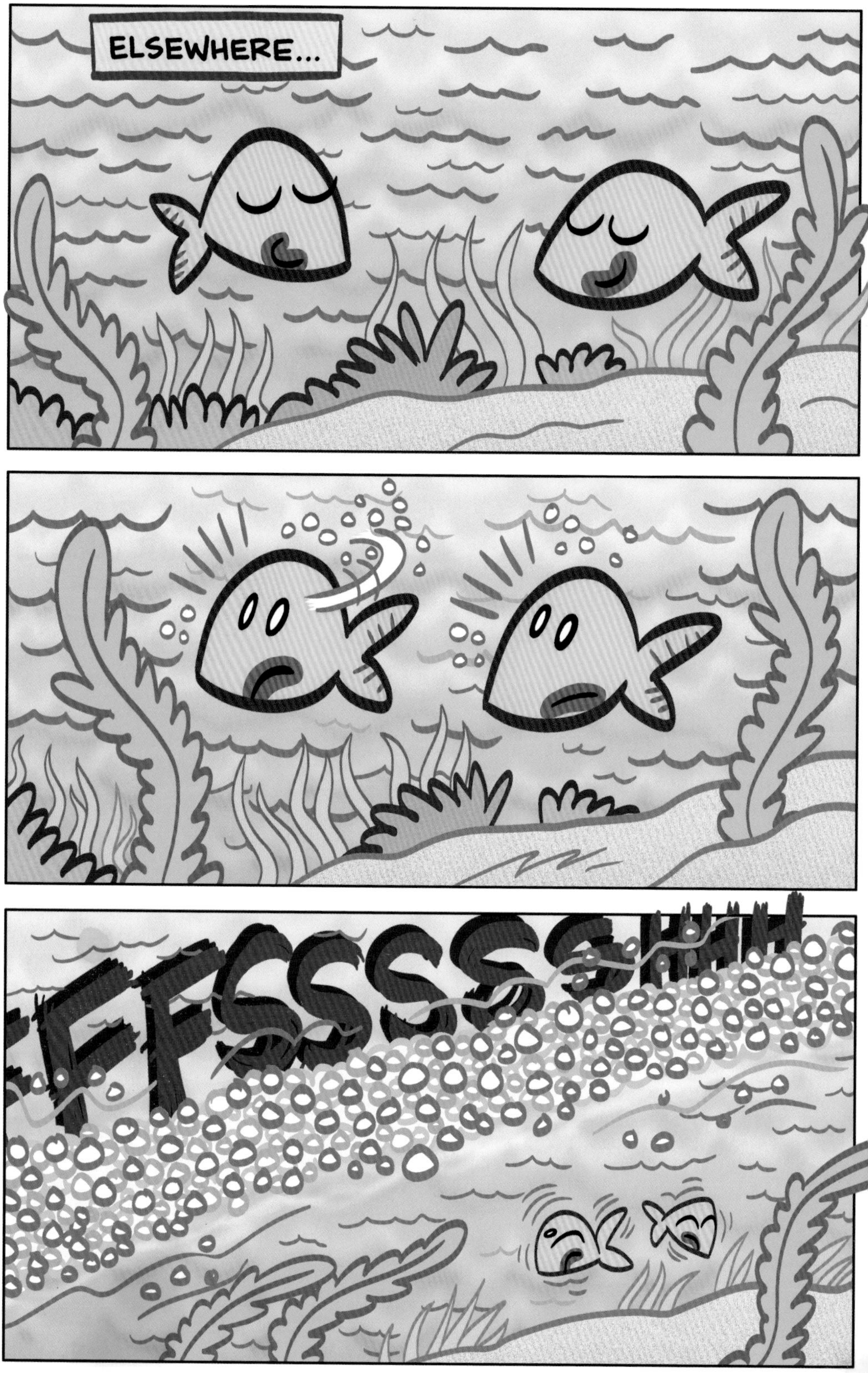
ELSEWHERE...
FFSSSSSHHH

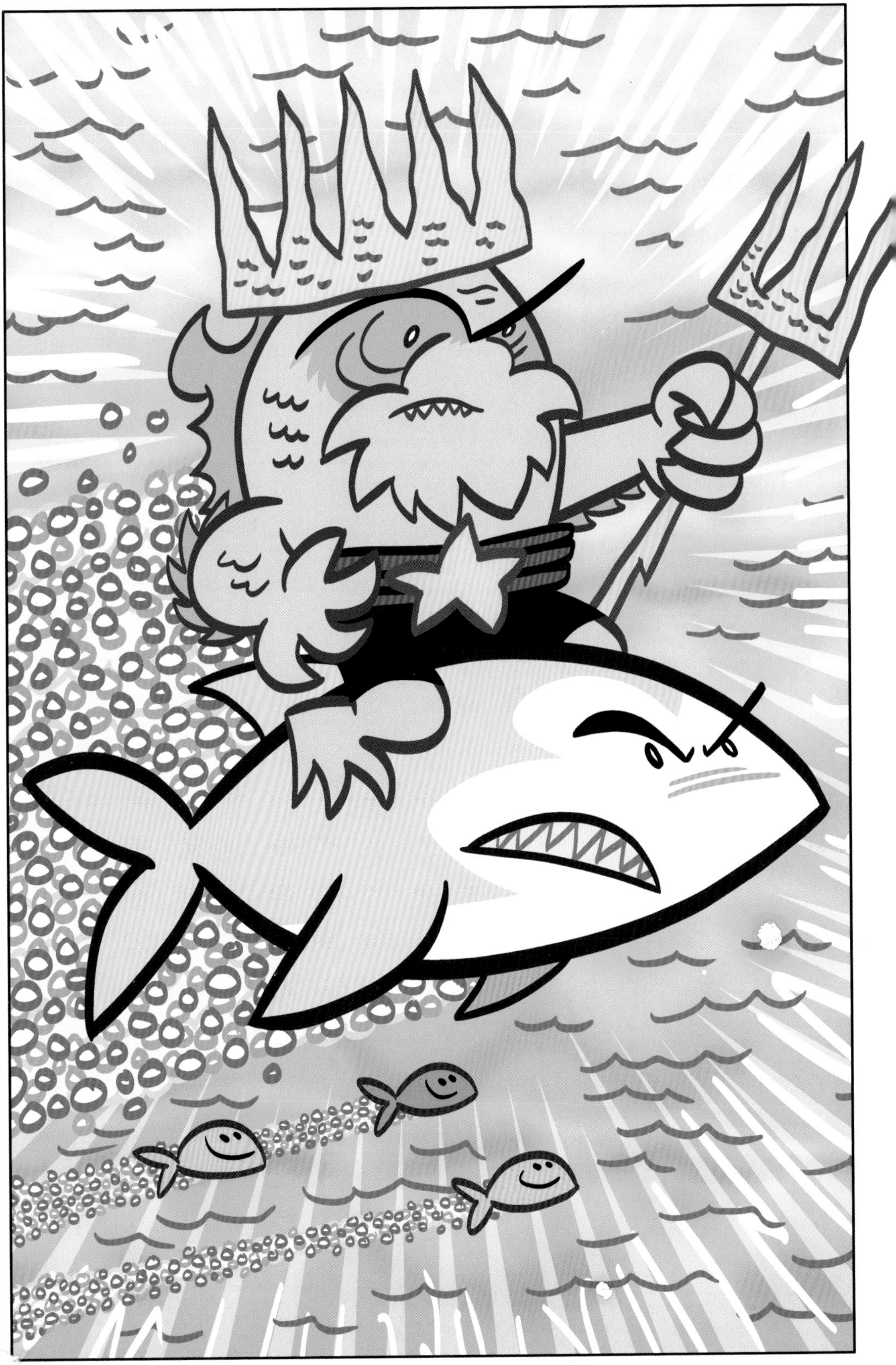

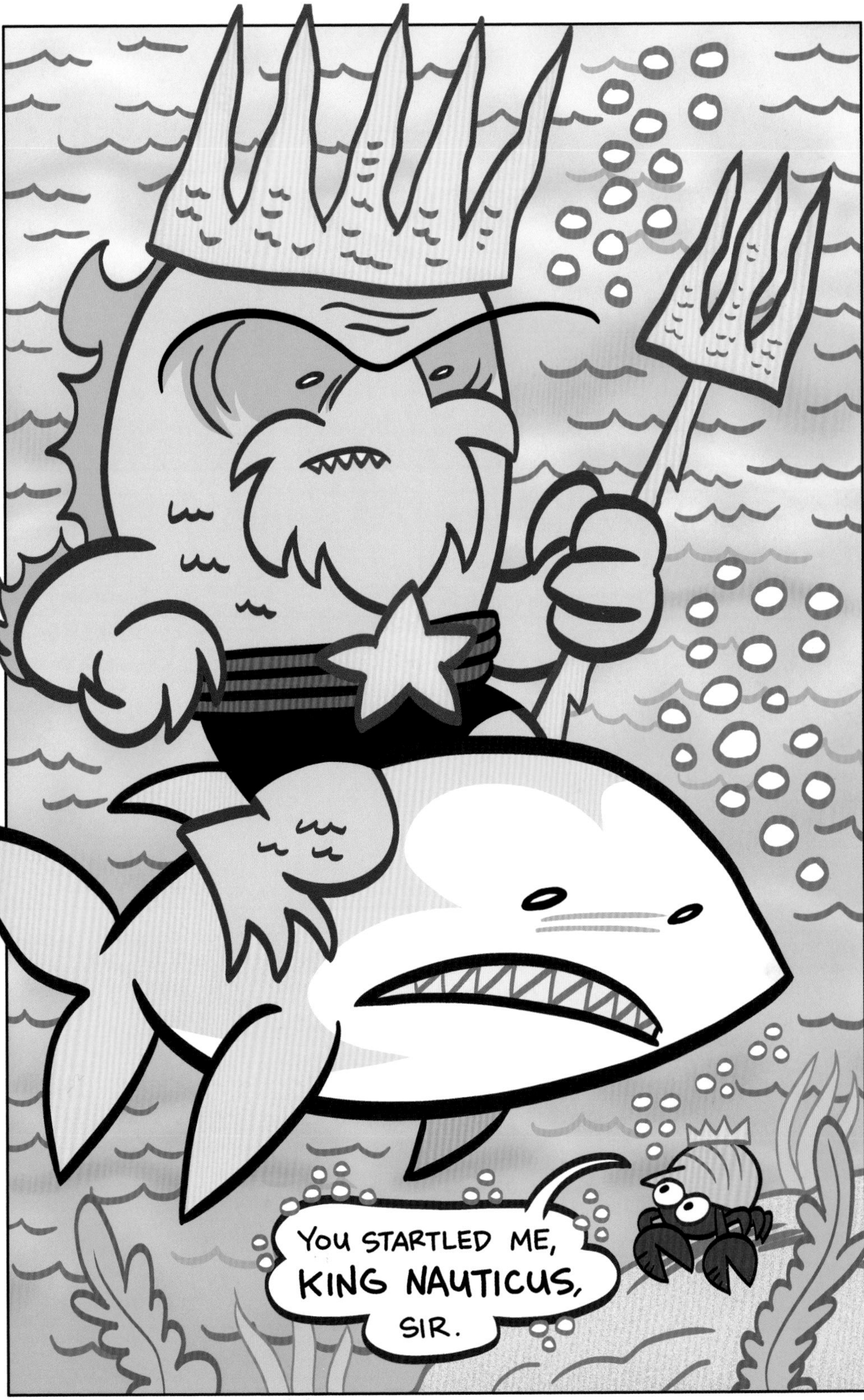
YOU STARTLED ME, KING NAUTICUS, SIR.

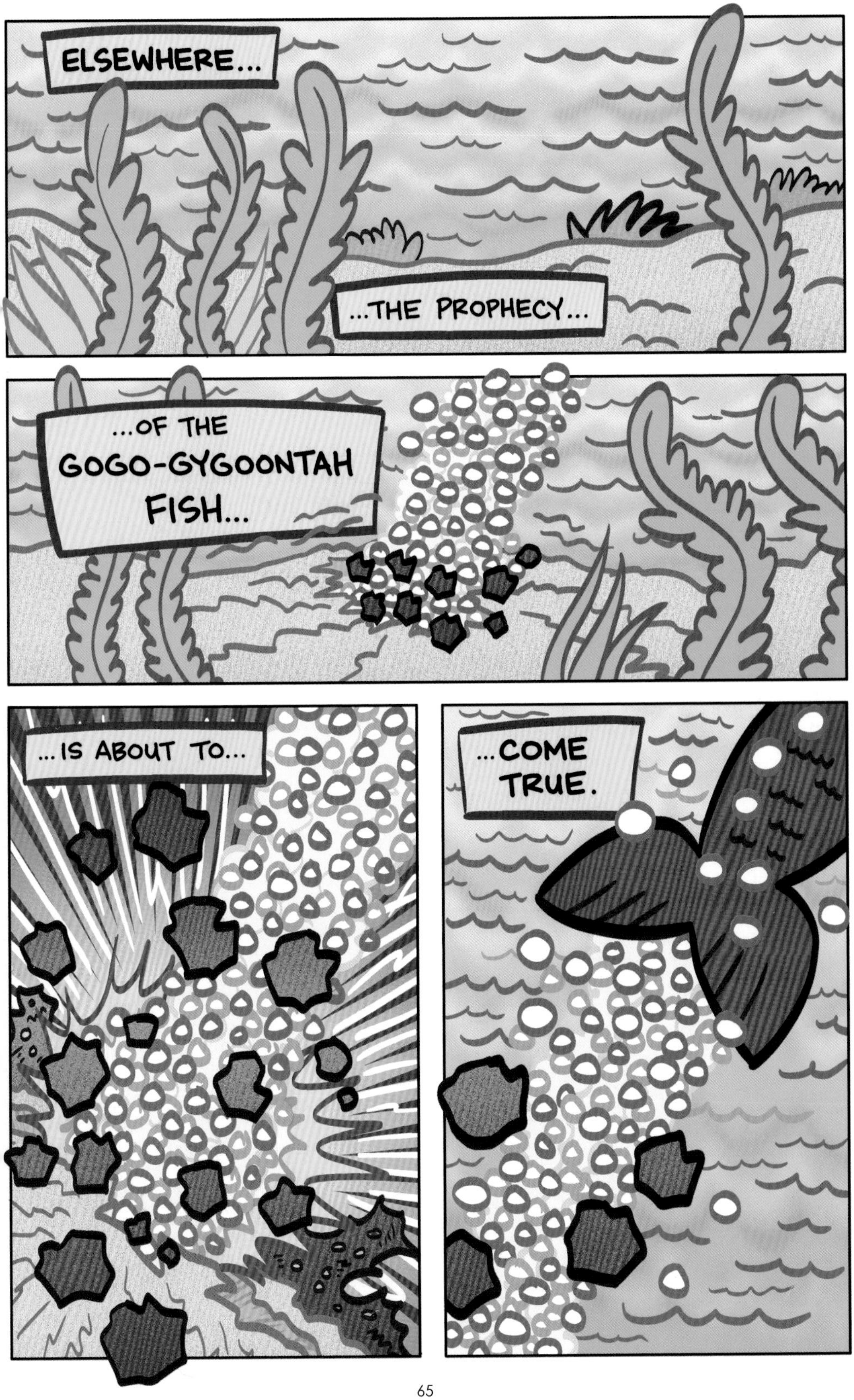
ELSEWHERE...
...THE PROPHECY...
...OF THE GOGO-GYGOONTAH FISH...
...IS ABOUT TO...
...COME TRUE.

69

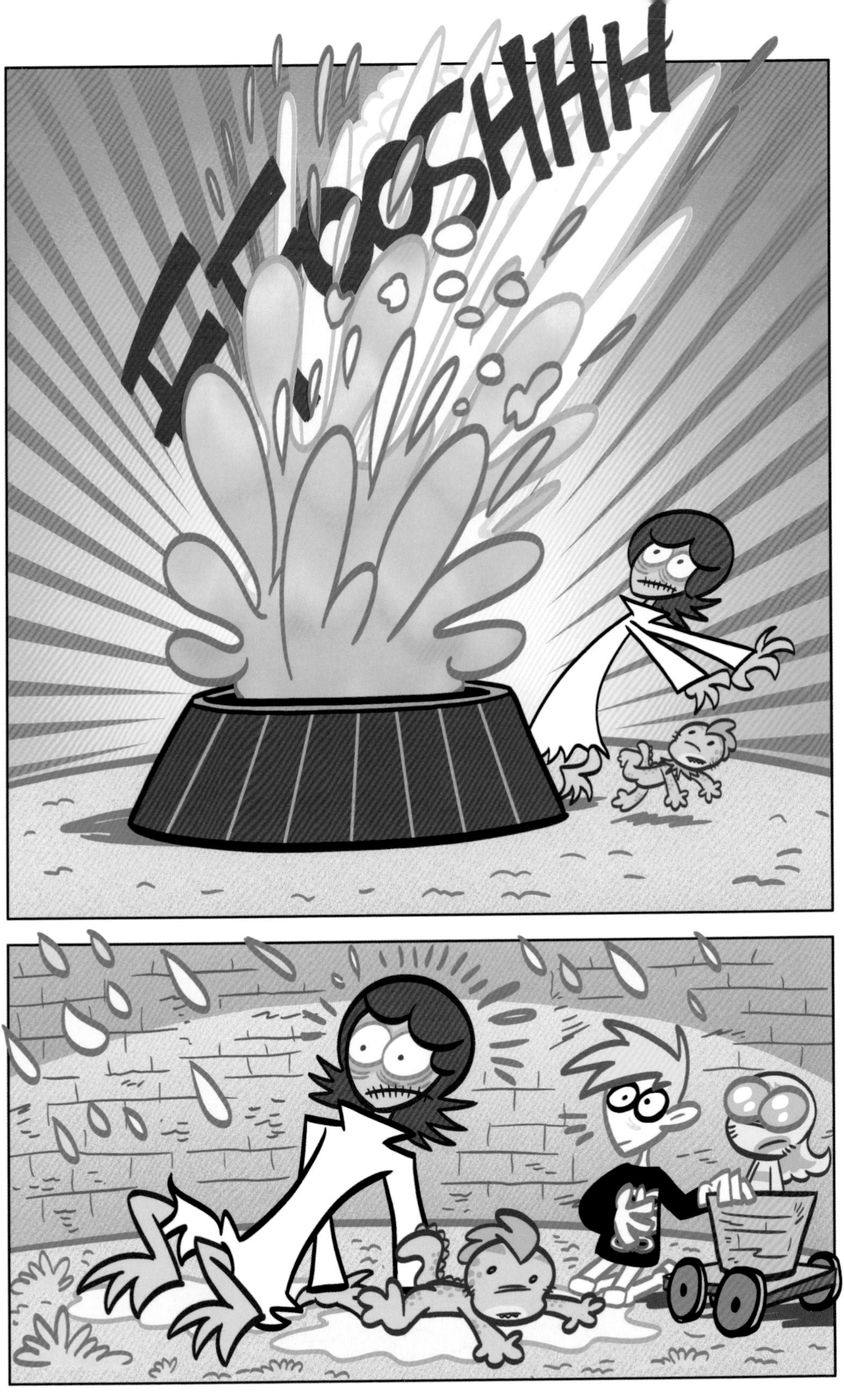
FTOOSHHH

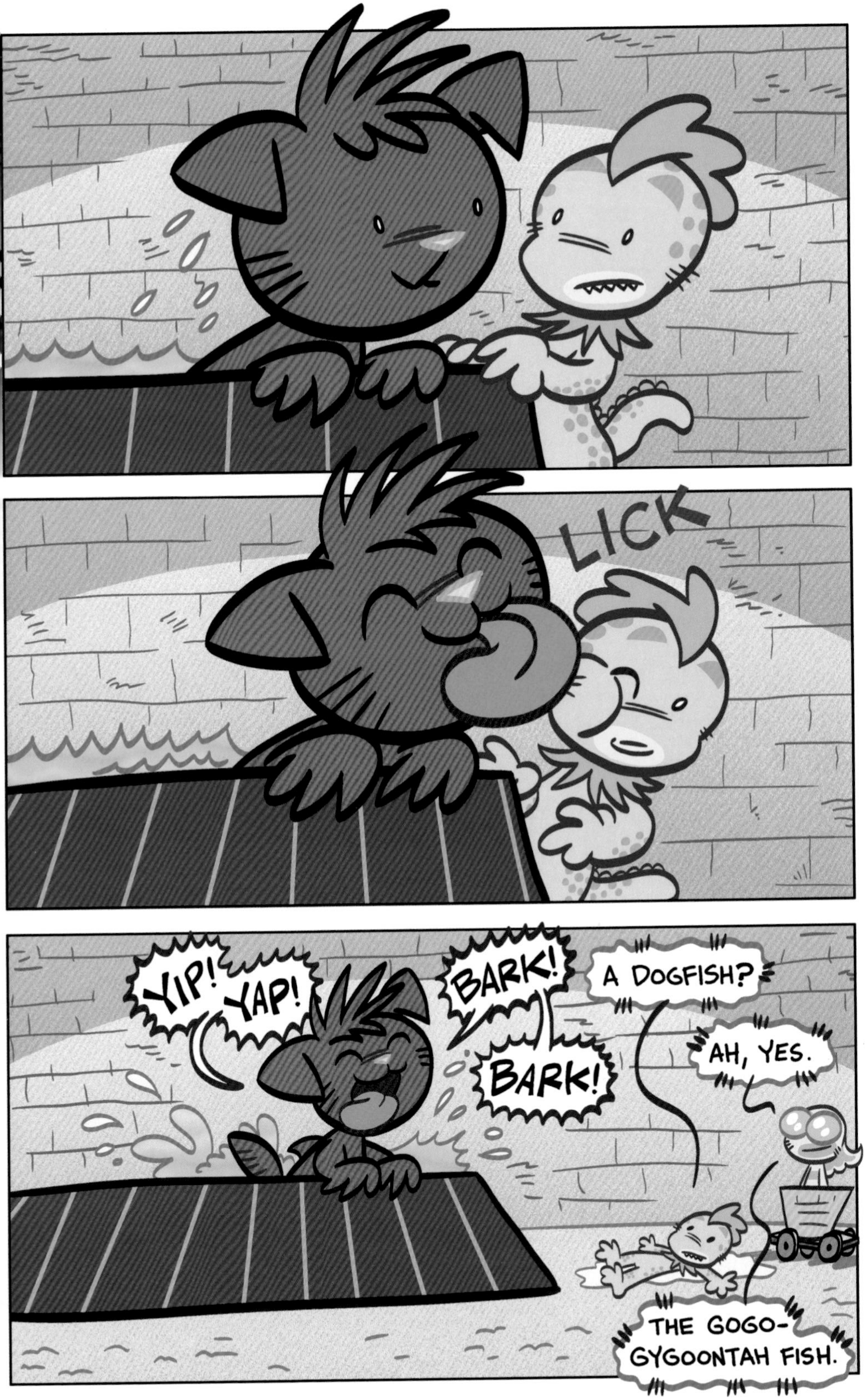
LICK
YIP!
YAP!
BARK!
BARK!
A DOGFISH?
AH, YES.
THE GOGO-GYGOONTAH FISH.

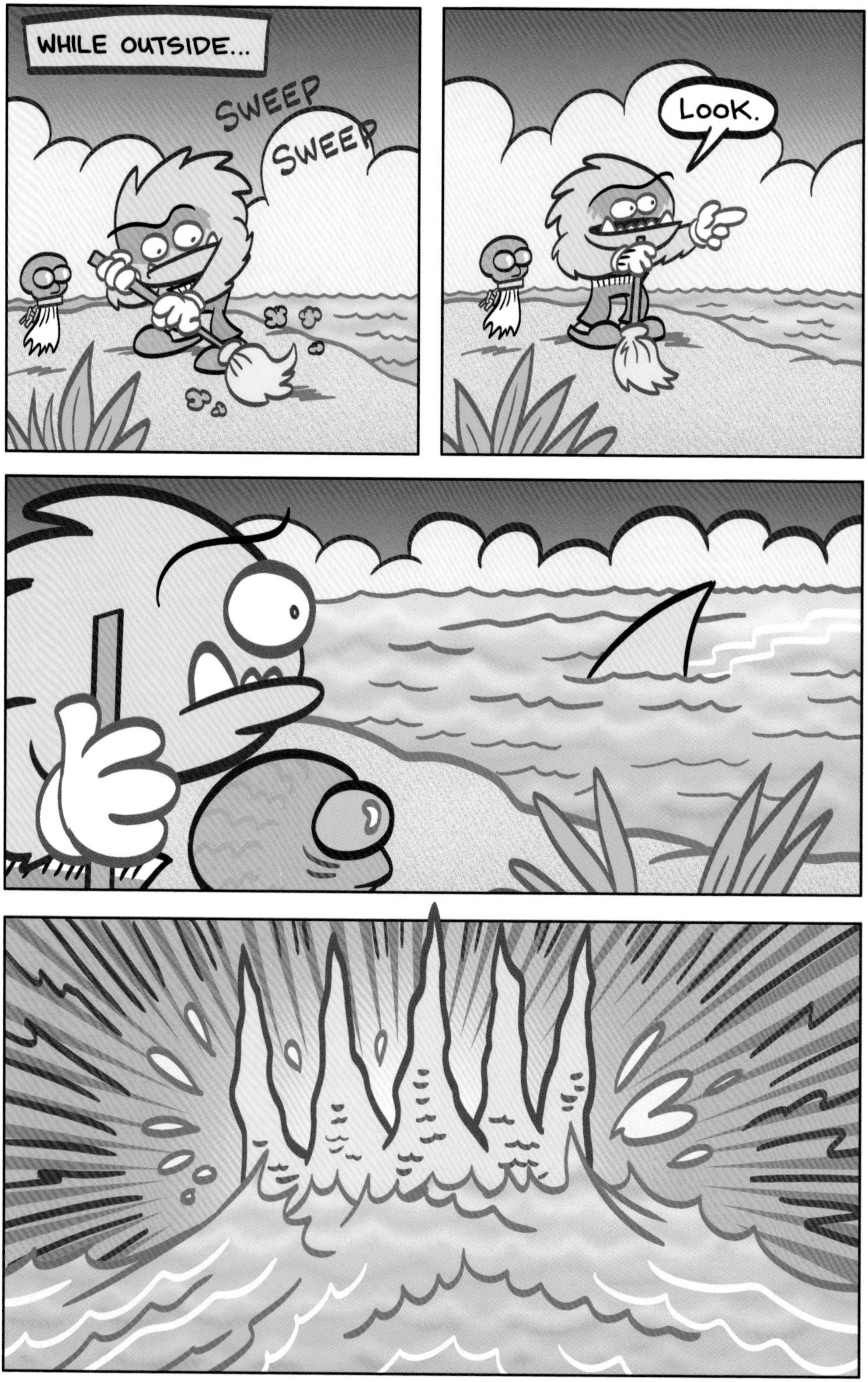
WHILE OUTSIDE...
SWEEP
SWEEP
LOOK.

-EVERYTHING IS EVERYTHING

WATCH OUT FOR PAPERCUTZ

Welcome to the second scaly and slippery volume of GILLBERT as we delve into "The Curious Mysterious" and put on our party hats to celebrate Everything Day AND Anything Day. I'm Jim Salicrup, Editor-in-Chief and captain of the ship here at Papercutz. We at Papercutz are big fans of all things underwater. In GILLBERT #1 we did mention Metaphrog's THE LITTLE MERMAID and David Gallaher and Steve Ellis's THE ONLY LIVING BOY. We have a confession to make, I am allergic to shellfish and our Managing Editor won't eat anything with fish in it except New England Clam Chowder. How curious and mysterious! Nevertheless, Papercutz has you covered for all your underwater book needs.

What's that? You enjoyed the Mostly Humans and their fun brand of horror? Well, Papercutz again has you covered! Join vampire Mavis, her husband Johnny, and her dad Dracula. THAT Dracula. The owner of HOTEL TRANSYLVANIA! Straight from the hit animated movies and Disney Channel series comes all-new adventures of the hotel and its ghoulish guests! Grab the three spooktacular volumes today before they disappear!

If you want your horror fun with a mix of romance, check out STITCHED from our Charmz imprint. Crimson Volania Mulch is piecing together her past as she wakes up in a cemetery uncertain of who she is or where she came from. While she is working on herself, she meets some great friends in a vampire, a werewolf, a not so mad scientist, and a sea creature! Volumes one and two are available wherever books are sold.

Lastly, also from Charmz, comes GFFs: GHOST FRIENDS FOREVER. Between high school, dealing with her stubborn twin brother, Felix, and her ex-boyfriend Jake, and the family business of ghost hunting, Sophia Green-Campos knows ghosts. But nothing can prepare her for meeting Whitney, a ghost who died in high school. This heartwarming tale of romance and family is available in two volumes.

Not creepy and not all-wet is GILLBERT's creator, Art Baltazar! Art Baltazar has been creating comics since 1994. Art calls his Art Studio (get it?) Electric Milk Creations. Among his hundreds of character creations and worlds, Art has been work-shopping GILLBERT and his dad, King Nauticus, since 2001! Turn the page for a special feature on the creation process for GILLBERT and the Mostly Humans! And watch the seas later this year for GILLBERT #3 "The Flaming Carats Evolution" but you might not want to get your books wet! Now, if you will excuse us, we have a Do It All Again Day to prepare for. It's tomorrow, you know!

Thanks,
Jim

STAY IN TOUCH!

EMAIL: salicrup@papercutz.com
WEB: papercutz.com
TWITTER: @papercutzgn
INSTAGRAM: @papercutzgn
FACEBOOK: PAPERCUTZGRAPHICNOVELS
FAN MAIL: Papercutz, 160 Broadway, Suite 700, East Wing, New York, NY 10038

Gillbert's first comic pitch!

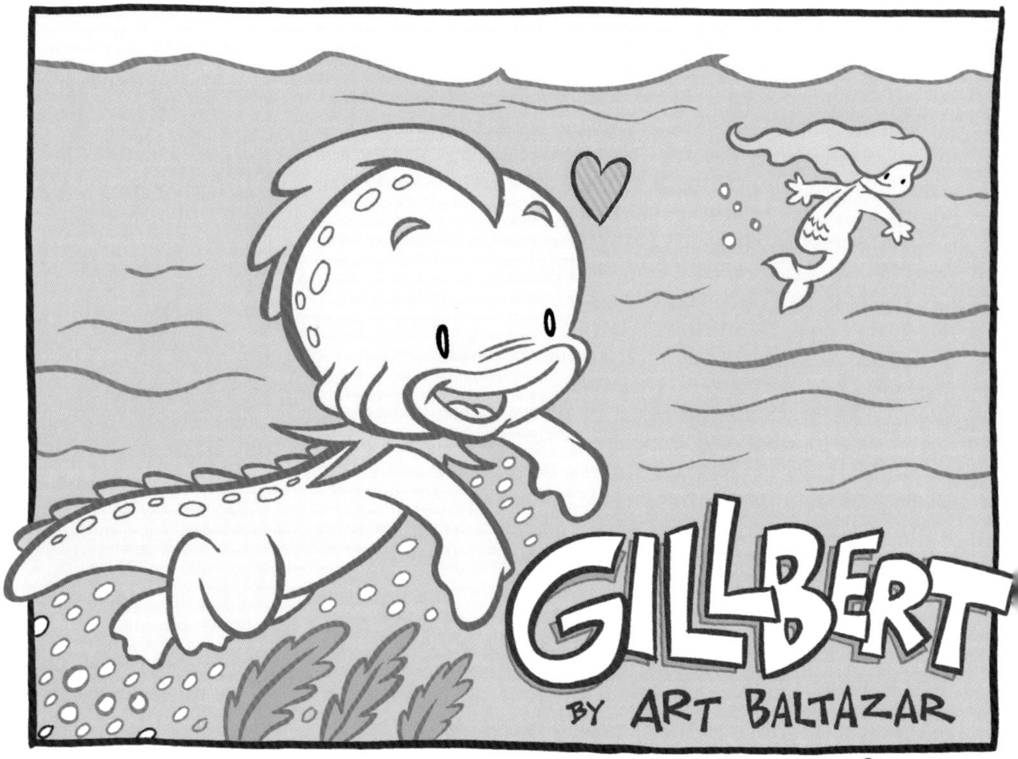
GILLBERT
BY ART BALTAZAR

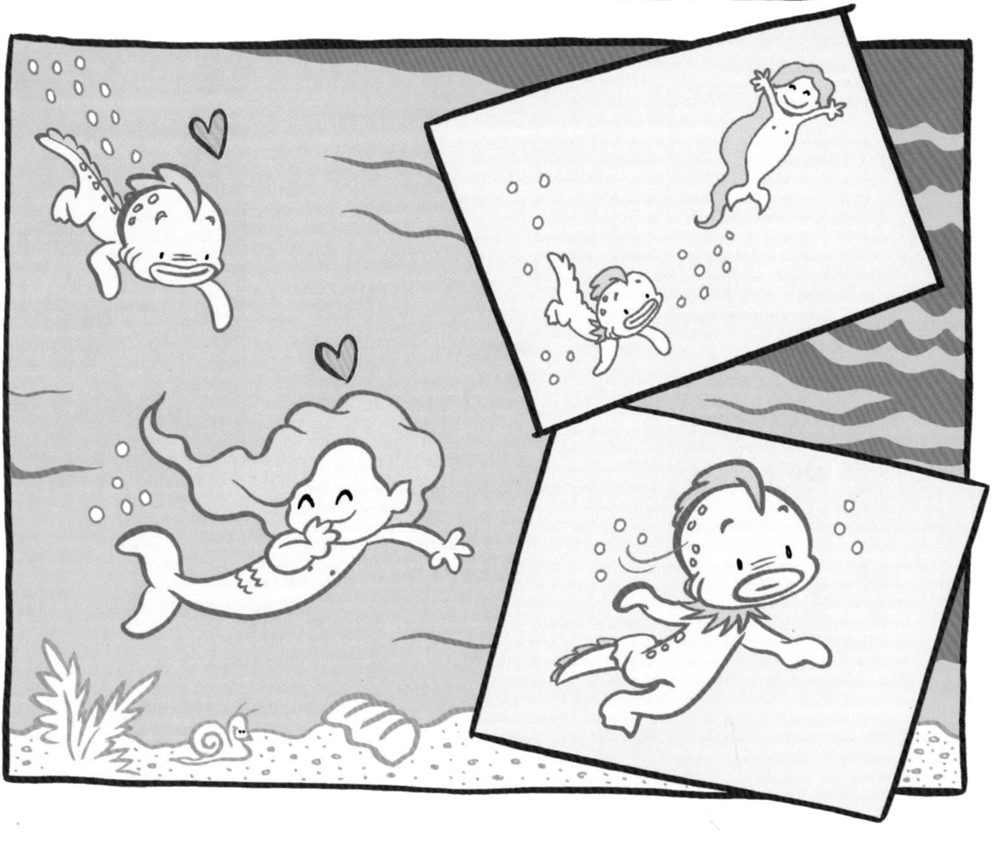

Famous cartoonist Art Baltazar has created hundreds of characters and given an Eisner Award-winning spin on classic comicbook properties like HELLBOY, TEEN TITANS, and the gang at ARCHIE. Art always keeps a sketchbook with him to be ready when inspiration hits. In 2001, he had an idea for a cute sea monster boy...

But Gillbert was not always destined for royalty. Allow us to explain. Art first created a creepy tragic tale of Doctor Wayne. You can read his creepy silent Wayne comic story at artbaltazar.com. Then, Art created a special school summer camp for Doctor Wayne to teach at, or to conduct experiments at. Art filled the school with some mostly human characters....

Art describes it this way: "While other kids go to summer camp, 'Gifted' kids attend Ms. Wayne's 'special' school. Come and visit the school where monsters are residents and Mad-Scientist experiments are a must. Years ago, Ms. Wayne lost her husband in a freak accident. Being a scientist, she tried and tried to bring her husband back from the dead."

GILLBERT

Art Batlazar's first sketches of GILLBERT, circa 2001

Art named the group "LABCOAT JUNCTION." Look familiar? At Labcoat Junction, the students are trained in the ways of a mad scientist and also how to care for, train, and live amongst monsters. What monsters you ask? Here they are:

So, that is the circle of creation. GILLBERT #1 "The Little Merman" premiered in 2018, 17 years after Art first created Gillbert! Now, the Mostly Humans have made their graphic novel debuts with

The Mostly Human(s) who Gillbert befriends in this volume. L to R: Wallace, Sonny Bone, LooEes the Beast , and Doctor Wayne,

GILLBERT #2 "The Curious Mysterious"! What surprises does Art Baltazar have in his sketchbook for volume 3? Only time will tell!

IT WAS GREAT MEETING YOU, MOSTLY HUMANS.

REMEMBER, GILL, THAT SEA CREATURE POSITION ON OUR TEAM IS ALWAYS OPEN.

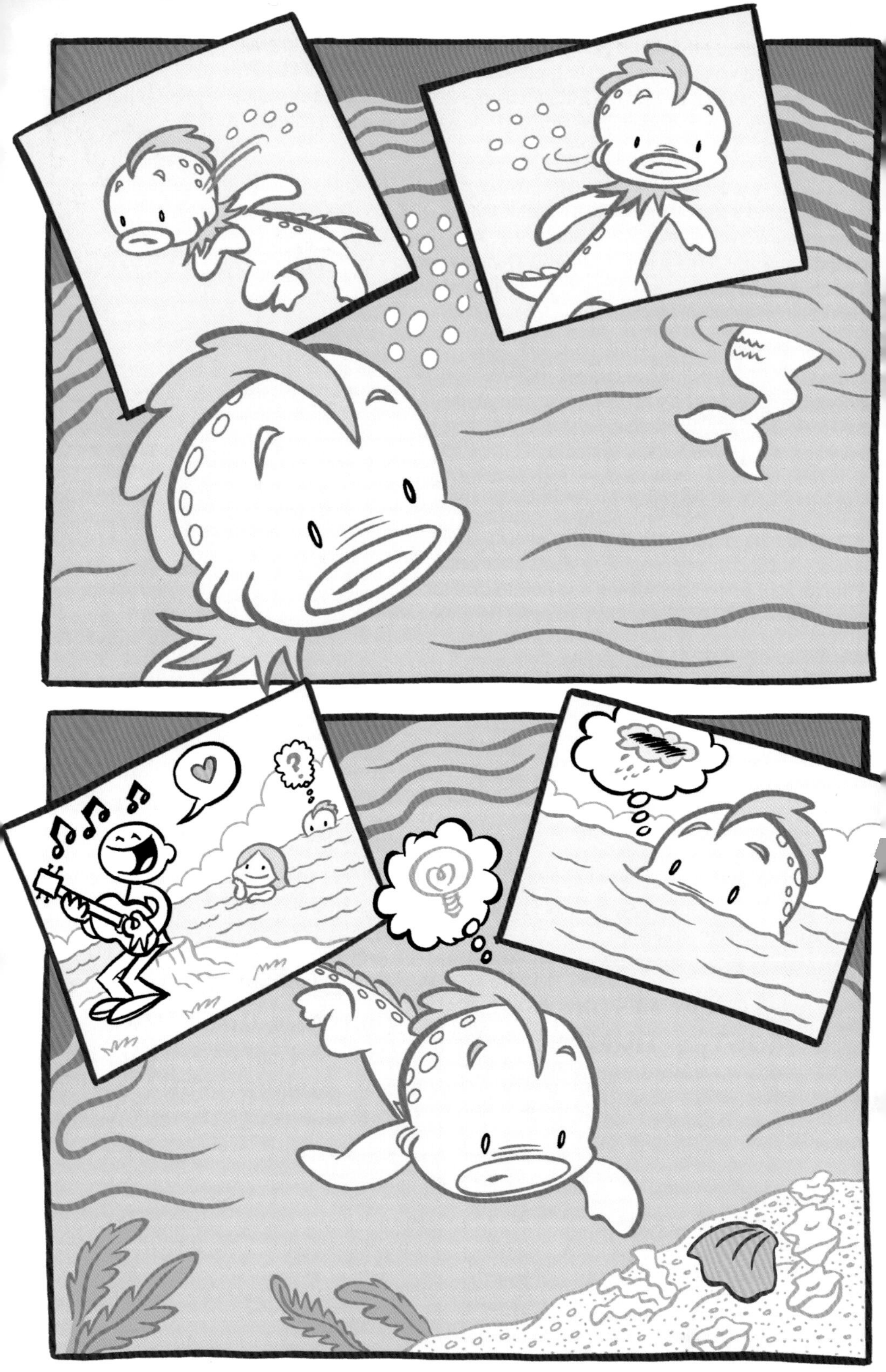

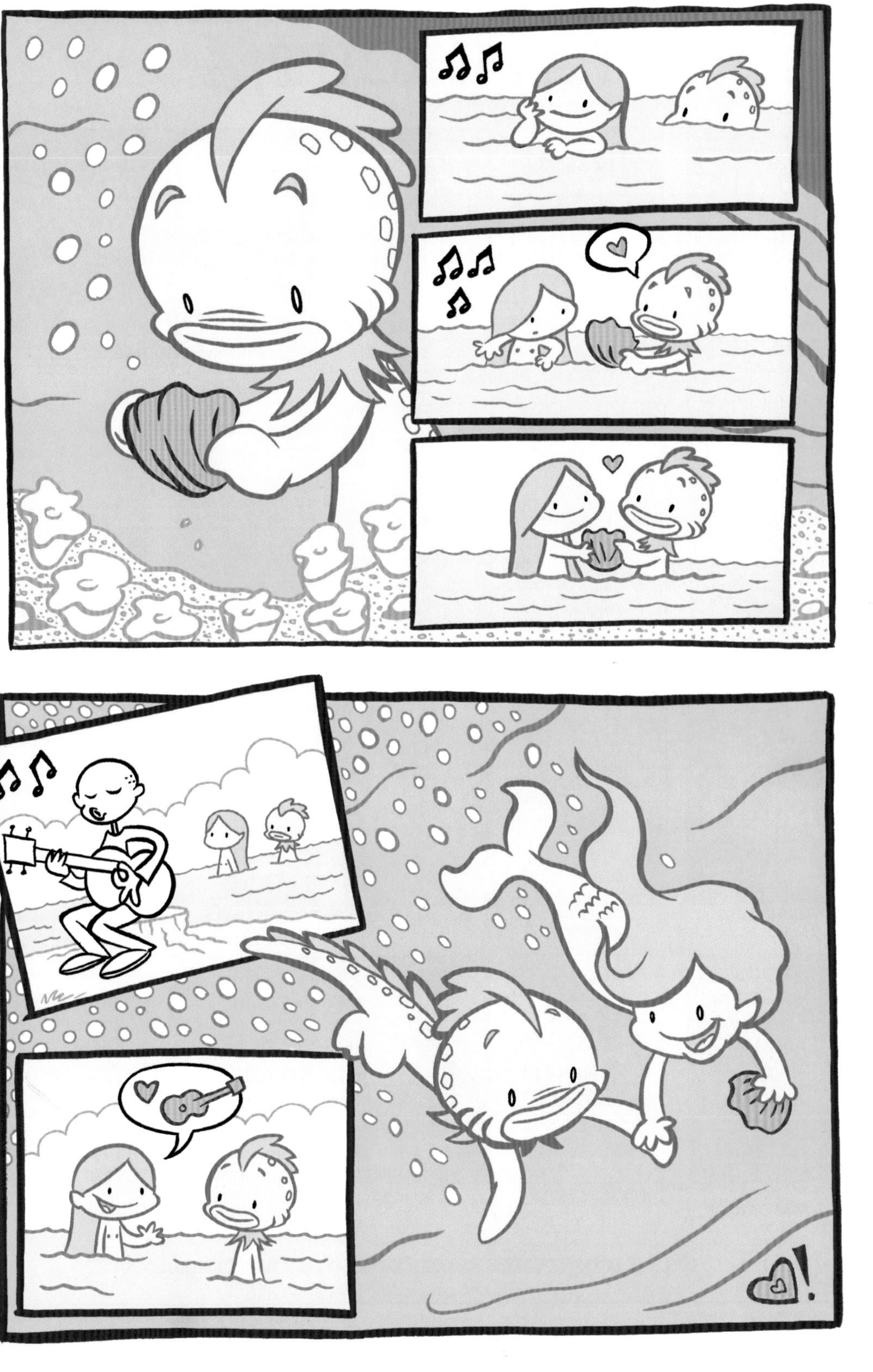

MORE GREAT GRAPHIC NOVEL SERIES AVAILABLE FROM

PAPERCUTZ™

THE SMURFS

GUMBY

BARBIE

THE SISTERS

CAT & CAT

GERONIMO STILTON

THEA STILTON

GERONIMO STILTON REPORTER

DINOSAUR EXPLORERS

BRINA THE CAT

THE MYTHICS

ATTACK OF THE STUFF

THE RED SHOES

THE LITTLE MERMAID

FUZZY BASEBALL

HOTEL TRANSYLVANIA

THE LOUD HOUSE

MANOSAURS

THE ONLY LIVING BOY

THE ONLY LIVING GIRL

Go to papercutz.com for more information
All available where ebooks are sold.

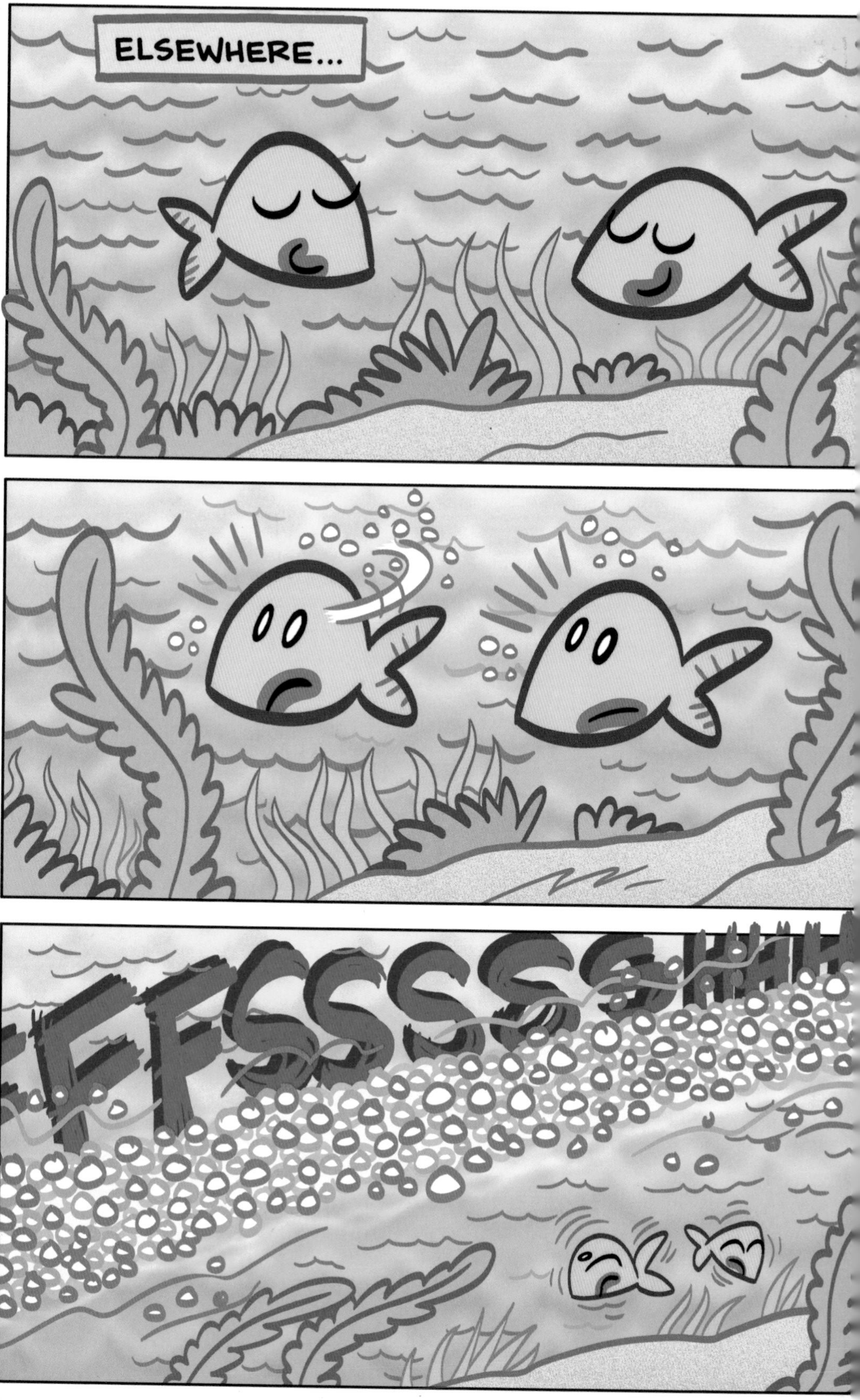
ELSEWHERE...
FFSSSSSHHH